To lovch

CW00455163

A TEACHER

A PRISON

A HOPE

GHOSTED

KATE DULSON

STRATOSPHERE BOOKS

ISBN: 978-1-8381611-9-4

Published by

Proofreader: Helen Woodhouse / phwproofreading.com

Original cover concept: Jonny Bainbridge / instagram.com/jonnybainbridge.art

Cover design and interior formatting: Mark Thomas / Coverness.com

To D – the words we promised each other we'd write.

1.

'Release for Labour and Education.'

The first to arrive slouches quickly into the chair nearest the door, hoping for a quick exit. I move to keep between him and the door. Just as I had been ordered to do. Just for the first few hours in any case. An amble of two more saunter in with raised eyebrows and mouths full of mischief.

'You're not the usual one.'

'Been sacked for giving us sweets, has she?'

'Are you going to be nicer? Bet you could be. The last one let us go early.'

'Pack it in. You know who she is. She told us yesterday. Didn't you see her watching us at the back?'

'What do you mean "watching"?'

And finally, the last face appears, scattering limbs and greetings before him.

'Been spun again. Didn't find anything though, did they? Made a right mess, they did. And did they tidy it up after? Messy bastards. And they say we're animals.'

The room struggles to expand, barely holding the rowdy comments thrown across it. The expectation has given way to chatter and gossip until the sound of the door banging shut stops play.

'Not sure you should do that, Miss. You don't know what we're like. We could be proper criminals.'

'Speak for yourself.'

Strained, mistrusting laughter.

In retrospect, having now seen his record, perhaps he was. But for now, let's be present. Deal with what I can see and not what could be imagined. Suspend all judgements. Not my job. That's already been done. And I would look daft in a white wig. Although silver streaks are creeping in. I'm feeling ridiculous as it is. How exactly did I end up here? A question mirrored in the silent, pale face in the corner. What the hell am I doing here? Let's start on basic and work our way up. Take a breath. Ready – never quite. Steady – almost never. Go.

'Right, let's begin. So today we are going to look at sentences.'

'Brilliant, Miss. I got four years.'

'Food farming? How many kilos?'

'Half a mil.'

'You got a touch.'

'And we all know what that weirdo is in for.'

Fuck. Fuck. Fuck. Fuck. Fuck. Fuck. Fuck.

'OK. Simmer down. Not that sort of sentence. I mean capital letters, punctuation and full stops.'

'Well, this has put a stop to being on road.'

'Shall we start again?'

Eyebrows raise a little. The pale face looks up. Longed-for silence.

'Well, that's what we're here for.'

'As soon as I'm back on road, I'm back to it.'

A worksheet later and they are rumbling, murmuring towards break.

'Can you mark mine, Miss?'

'I got more than you.'

'Didn't go to school, so why should I fuckin' do it now? Do alright. Makin' bare money.'

'And how's that working out for you?'

Slipped out. Slithered into the space in the centre of the room and crept under the desks. Pause. Weighing up options. Narrow stare returned with a smile and raised eyebrow.

'Fair point, Miss. Let's get this over with.'

Two hours later, they start to collect papers together to leave behind in a folder. Each one hands in their pen despite me not asking them to.

'Is it that time already?'

'Miss, you don't need to mention time. We know it. We're doing it, not you.'

'Actually, I can't retire for another twenty-eight years.'

'You could have killed four people and be out in less. My man only did five.'

'That's like half the class, Miss.'

Not quite the embedded maths I'd planned. Should we work

out the probability of me surviving a week? A month? Or the chances of them turning up tomorrow?

'Cease Labour and Education.'

Edging to be first out of the rickety wooden Education unit door. Noses pressed against film-covered glass, fingers poking out of human-hole-punched glass. A scatter of voices spreads outwards. Driftwood on a regular tide. The pale face looks back.

'See you tomorrow, Miss.'

I did miss him when he finally left with a string bag, ill-fitting court suit, and £50 in his drooping pockets. Polyester skin clinging around old bones. His was the first story I heard. A walking textbook on the inhumanity of an IPP – a now outlawed indeterminate sentence. One without a clear end or full stop. He'd taken a handbag from under a café table, and twelve years later he was still inside. He'd been moved around, starved, bullied, and borne witness to more than he could whisper. His family had died without any goodbyes. Wearing a donated suit that hung its head with sorrow, the funeral escorts weren't even allowed to uncuff him. It broke all the rules. Abolished over ten years ago, I was choked to discover men still being held on IPPs. Hidden from sight, haunted relics of injustice masquerading as public protection. This museum was full of exhibits. But they were tricky to spot. Transparent, ashen skin pinched around mime-act eyes. Endless barbed wire coiled around dreams of leaving.

Stay behind me if you need to, but we are heading in. Pretend to walk beside me later on when you've heard what it's like from the spectators' gallery. Stay in the cheap seats where you can't quite catch the smell of blood and pasties. Don't head for the push-and-shove pit unless you've learnt the rules. Those regulatory training courses usefully scheduled after the first weeks of panic scorch the back of your throat. Pretend it's the rush, the thrill of crossing the line. Beyond this is where your worst fears are kept, the ones pushed from view into white G4 vans screeching from court before you can see how unreassuringly normal they look. The ones you have walked past, shaken hands with, worked with, perhaps loved or lost.

Stay awake. Stay safe. Push it back. Push it down under the barbed-wire comments you can hear muttering behind you. Focus on where we are. Watch the plastic bag leaves scurrying along the perimeter fence. Hide and seek where the light slips through the gaps as the sun squints from behind the duvet-crumpled clouds and thinks better of it for today. Wise move. It knows something we don't yet.

After a long drive through woods, farmland flat poppy fields, it's too late to turn back. Just a thin line of green lime trees left, which whispers my arrival at the high painted fences. Topped with barbed wire and flagged by warning signs: Dogs Patrol Here. A lone dog walker shuffles past with a regal greyhound in tow. It pees under the sign and walks on. This won't be the only time I step sideways to avoid a yellow trickle heading for my shoes. Mental note: always wear strong, wipeable shoes. Also useful for making a quick getaway if needed. We've reached the edge of your world.

The Union Jack flag flaps to stake its claim on no-man's-land. As I walk under it, eyes follow me before I'm lost inside the gatehouse. They scatter on black wings to announce another arrival ahead of the white G4 vans waiting at the barriers. Chattering spreads over the wings until they perch on landings, cackling. There's fresh meat at the door.

'Prohibited Items include: Guns, weapons, knives, sharp objects, foil, aerosols, chewing gum, drugs, alcohol, yeast, phones, cameras and recording devices, cigarettes, lighters. Anyone found in possession of these items could face a sentence of up to ten years in prison.'

And, as I learnt later: paper, old £20 notes, spiral-bound notebooks, charcoal, clay, oil paints, Blu-Tack, tape, staples, pens containing metal parts, personal photos, identification, prescription medicines, paracetamol, biscuits, food, more than £50, unapproved books, CDs, DVDs, any game or DVD with an 18+ rating, radios, glass items, metal cutlery, china plates, more than one piece of fruit, rubbers, playing cards, maps, timetables, tickets.

We're all sucked into the airlock. Uniformed and civilian. Wet hair from hasty showers, bloodshot eyes smile and joke until the door slides shut. Tighter lips and weaker smiles. We're heading in. Jostling to keep within the lines, a few in-jibes are shared. Liverpool lost last night. Scouser will be keeping his head down. Air sits at the back of my throat until we are spat out on the other side.

It's time to get into character now. For the first few days I was collected and escorted by a colleague. Just a watcher at the back of the class. Now I have been trained on how to use a radio and collect my keys, I have to navigate the black and white sea alone. Collect a heavy bunch of large keys, Victorian and modern. I still walk with tilted hips. Try not to set off the alarms. Again. Put the keys on my belt and in a pouch out of sight. The only place I can't carry my keys is in my fist. If they are on view I will be walked out, never to return. Do not pass Go. Do not collect £200. No Get Out of Jail Free card. That exit will be a costly one. Collect a radio. Check it has a battery with at least half charge. That will take me to lunchtime. Link it on my belt holder. Put in the earpiece and snap it onto my ear. Now I can hear everything: announcements, calls for assistance, codes in colours. Check they know which radio I have. Just in case they need to find me if I can't speak. Push past the anxious eyes checking rotas. My routine is comfortingly the same, but without the respect from a uniform. Find the right key. Unlock the gate. Don't be nice. Stop being that little bit more human. Don't hold it open for anyone. Bang it shut. Keys out of sight. Check it. Push check it. Get laughed at by the older and wiser officers. Smile back. Watch their reaction. At best, a smile returned. At worst, an eye roll for the incoming snowflake.

The night staff pass by, murmuring of unrest and fifteen-minute bed watches. Above me, the rooks are laughing. At least it isn't a murder of crows. At least the ducks seem perkier this morning. Behind their own compound fence, the newly christened Dave falls silent when Chinese meals are mentioned.

He has also heard the stories of how to cook a pigeon in a kettle. I pull my bag closer. A small clutch purse stripped of all personal items. Tip toe over the slimy paths which have claimed a few recently. Best not to fall base over apex in front of a reception wing full of men.

It's 7.00 a.m. but most of the residents are already awake. Staring through slits or passing items between cells via mugs on string. The rooks watch the ketchup tennis as a bottle is swung between cells across the outside of Induction Wing. Red-stained walls evidence a few escape attempts until it reaches the last cell on the right.

'Morning, Miss.'

'Morning, Kate.'

'Haven't seen you before.'

'Morning. See you later.'

'Am I on a promise then?'

I remember his voice from yesterday's wing tour.

'Sam, I am old enough to be your mother. I feel like your grandmother if we're honest. We've talked about this.'

'I know, Miss. But I am inside. Tends to make me a bit desperate. Lower me standards, like.'

The door to the unit sighs shut. Tutting as the lock wobbles, our joints creak a little more today. In spite of myself, I smile unseen. The false optimism. Of Living the Dream. Another Day in Paradise begins in earnest.

After a quick coffee in the staff room, we lock the managers safely in their office unit and go to our classrooms. Mine is reassuringly opposite the admin offices, within sightlines. Being at the top of the stairwell, the grey sea of men washes by each morning. A different weary tide in the afternoon. There are windows, which open a little. The universal law of classrooms still applies – either arctic or the temperature of the surface of the sun.

Chairs under tables. Just seven chairs to begin with. The number of men is always different. First solo lesson without a mentor. My second prison class. Still in Freshers' Week. But stone-pale, cold, and very sober. Cold enough to see your breath outside and only a little warmer inside. Catching dragon breaths. Picking one out of the air and holding it before a shaky release. Prickling fingers hastily arrange the papers and best-laid plans. Work around the inside, arrange a single, lidless pen next to a battered dictionary, and wait for the signal.

'Lock 'em up and throw away the key.'

'What?'

'Oh, you heard. You won't make me change my mind. They have free TV, three hot meals, and a hot shower every day. Should swap them with our elderly in the care homes. Disgusting.'

'You can't say that. That's what you've seen in the papers. It's really not true.'

'It is. I've seen the photos of takeaway wrappers in the bins. They have a life of luxury.'

'That's actually when we ran out of plates. They cropped the bean-sodden slime from the edges of the boxes.'

'Well, they don't deserve decent food.'

'For fuck's sake, Lynne. Is it any wonder the others call you "Karen" behind your back? Are you really going to complain to the manager? If you could see what I feel and smell every day, you might just change your mind.'

'You wouldn't get me anywhere near that sort of place.' She shovels the last of her smashed avocado into her mouth before continuing. 'I just couldn't do what you do.'

'No one is asking you to. Sometimes, on the worst days, I wonder why I do. Not everyone can handle it. One teacher only lasted until lunchtime.'

'I don't know why you do it: go in there.' A pause. Here it comes. 'You must have some stories.'

'I have a few. None of them include hot showers or meals though.'

'No? Go on. Tell me. What's it really like working in prison?'

I have already clocked the ears pricking at the next café table. Pretending not to listen in. They're taking a very long time over that chai latte. Should have ordered an iced one. Cold comfort if they could see the stories I can't tell. I've got over the initial thrill of saying I work in a prison. That crept away like the trickling cold shower water through cracked tiles. Now I am a keeper of stories which aren't just my own. All names have been changed to protect the guilty. I include myself somewhere in that.

'I don't know what to tell you. You can't unhear some things.'

'You're so selfish, keeping the juicy stuff to yourself. What's the good of knowing someone on the inside if you can't enjoy the drama?'

The combination of the smell of burnt toast and kitchen alarm has sent me back there. I'm already on my guard, scanning the people close by and listening for the orders to leave. It should be OK. I've picked a spot by the door with my back to the wall, despite Lynne moaning that she wanted to sit outside and people-watch.

'If it's drama you want, that I can give you. Stories you wouldn't believe.'

'Ooh, try me!'

So I take to the stage. Tell her just enough about dead rats filled with drugs and phones. Nothing that hasn't already been in the news or edited trauma-porn documentaries. Staff chasing drones across fields, barricades, bomb scares, riots of laughter and kindness. She doesn't like those hopeful tales. Her lip curls and they don't sit right in her hardened stomach. So I return to the tales she could easily read in the papers. Drugs and fights. But there just aren't enough of them. Holding men apart is always followed by holding men together. Holding myself together.

She continues her interrogation.

'Have you met anyone famous? Anyone I would have heard of?'

I know she is an avid fan of lurid documentaries, gobbling

down transcripts and swallowing lies. But I can't tell her the truth, let alone the whole truth. Those lies are caught on the perimeter fence, high wire fingers holding on.

'Yes. I have. You'd know their names if I said them. But you know I won't. They aren't my stories to tell.'

'Oh, go on . . .'

For a second I almost let a name from this week slip. Of how he told me how to dismantle a particular item from my dad's house, which would identify him here. The ridiculous moment of fate that put me briefly in the same room as the someone who would actually know how to stop me smashing the stupid relic up. She also wouldn't believe I knew and respected men who shared Broadmoor meals with a man who had terrorised a generation of women across two counties. A man who took away my love of the Northern night, pushed me into anxious parents' cars, and cut short evenings of joy and community.

'If I told you, I'd have to kill you.'

She smiles. 'I'm sure you'll tell me some other time, Kate. When you're ready.'

An image of officers crying in their parked cars before driving home flickers across my cold tea. Strong, cold Yorkshire Tea. My reflection slips between swirls, held by porcelain edges.

I don't think I will ever be ready. I'm not sure how long the danger will take to dissolve into the sludge at the bottom of my cup. Dredging it, slipping through my fingers as I write. I'm holding onto quicksand, falling through safety nets. Gang leaders had already let me know they knew where I lived. How many children I have. I still park a safe distance from the school gates as my grumpy children push past the pusher soldiers on bikes to slump into the car.

'I won't. You wouldn't want to walk a mile in my shoes.'

'Agreed. They are pretty tatty, darling. Let's get you some more. Break's over and we're missing good shopping time!'

And off we whirl. I let her carry me in her wake, a sea of shoppers ploughed by bags of floating shoes and strappy sandals. She is a force of nature, enviably oblivious to the stabbing sight of shop staff radios and security guards following us. In the rush to kick off the mud masking piss-bloody boots, I had forgotten to take off my work belt. The metal chain has already triggered two shop alarms. Luckily, one security team is led by a familiar face. Lynne misses our quick glances of recognition.

'Causing trouble again, Miss?' as he smiles us through.

Her frenzied surge towards the sale rack of designer dresses means she doesn't see me still musing over seeing Dan. Quiet acknowledgement belies another dangling label. A clinging, sticky jam jar label which never soaks off: ex-offender. I think about ways to acknowledge him fully without giving the game away. Seeing him on the outside warms my evening more than the orange shoes I will never wear.

It was a mistake. Both the shoes and the late-night shopping trip. I woke up crumpled from a sofa coma ten minutes before John arrived outside.

'Fuck. Fuck. Fuck. Fuck.' More Four Funerals and No Wedding.

I hurtle upstairs to grab a different dull dress because they will notice if I rock up in the same one as yesterday. Pulling it off, the faint whiff of perfume and blood from holding Adam's wounds trails past my nostrils. No time to recoil even if it hadn't become normal. Pinging a dress from a hanger, which flick-spits its disgust back before clattering to the floor, I mutter 'Sorry' to the heap of mardy duvet turning away from the light. He stirs but there is only no rest for the wicked. I pull on the dress and dash to the door.

John pulls up in his wife's little coupé. He already knows what kind of day it will be. What he doesn't realise is how this lift share lifeline carries me through. No way of going back or pulling a sickie. He laughs, raised eyebrows as I crunch, wincing, barefoot on gravel to collect the crusty boots from where they had been thrown in the car boot.

'Mornin.'

'Sadly, it is.'

'You might want to clean that off.'

Toothpaste dribble down my less than ample cleavage now smeared like windscreen bird shit, and we are off into the sunrise. Only, I'm already there. The sharp stones pull me forward to the grit and bark chippings that always find a way to announce the gatehouse.

'How do you do it?'

'What?'

'You know. Doing this job. Turning up. Not letting it show.'

'It's a job. OK money. Leave it all at the gate.'

'You can do that? When does that superpower kick in?'

'Pfft! We ain't paid enough to do homework.'

'True. People still ask me how much the danger money is.'

'Just play the game, never show your cards.'

'Ah. Not sure I have the right pack. Mine are all jokers.'

'Never play poker for money either.'

'Did you know about the playing cards thing?'

'Yes.'

'Oh. Of course you have. Is nothing sacred, eh?'

Mundane objects act like lurching rogue time machines. Playing cards signal drug orders from pack menus. Causing chaos to the poker schools who need them just as much. The vape coiling smoke tendrils pull me back. From high street to cell in a second. Burnt toast spun to canteen day. Yells over bean pools slipping off plates. Shop alarms throw me forward.

Spiralling spaces and time fix upon moments held by routine. Tomorrow will be another day. Yet another day of the same but different. The courses revolve on either a four- or six-week basis. This airport conveyor belt spits out the unclaimed ones, the returners who have nowhere to go. Some explode, spilling their guts to jam the machine. Others remain tight shut, strapped in, and locked. Buckle up, it will be a bumpy ride driving towards danger or the quick getaway careering through country lanes. A new life of opposing forces, shape-shifting, changing for better and worse. A marriage made in no hope in hell. But a work husband was a find. A shiny, bald diamond in the rough. More priest than partner really, especially as there was nothing else going on. Four hours in a car each day is a lengthy confession broken up by splintered stories, silences, jokes, and covering the bloodstains with comforting, dull tales of family life.

2.

After the initial baptism of fire, things seemed to settle. A training sequence shortened. No longer lingering in the dark mornings before time stops as the front door shuts behind me. Whispering 'don't leave' as it rolls over to hold the duvet edges of my family together. After all, the only time I had actually been assaulted was as a young university lecturer. Now twenty years older, I thought I was wiser if saggier. Exchanging dreaming spires for barbed insomnia wires, this wasn't quite the 'Butlin's' atmosphere Lynne and I had been promised by her *Daily Mail*. I'd read the newspapers claiming that prisons were either holiday camps or training schemes for future career criminals. Dubbed 'the universities of crime', I began to feel at home. Here were the mustard yellow doors of my childhood, strict regimes, and the semblance of order. But here I have the keys. And, as an added bonus, there was no homework to mark. No helicopter parents (or so I thought). No officer in the building, let alone in the classroom to remind me of where I was. Missing in action elsewhere.

I hear voices in my earpiece, speaking of incidents and alerts. Of fights and first aid needed. I wanted to turn down these announcements – my ears pinch in pain – but we have to hear what is happening around us. An incident may not be contained on a wing for long. There were fights outside that meant we couldn't finish classes and had to keep the men indoors. Beyond their dinner time. Beyond meds time. This always incited a heady mix of rage and humour.

'If I miss *Hollyoaks,* I will be fuckin' livid.'

'No danger of that, my son.'

The door is forced again and they run out. Anxious to get the last of the sloppy canteen food before it becomes a brown-ringer.

Worse than the ringing in my ears – which is now constant, earpiece or not – is the silence between calls for extra support and the order to stand down. After the initial call, officers would run to the source and all wings were locked down. Even if it was time for medication at Health Care. No one moved between buildings. My body and brain have learnt to carry on teaching, handing out worksheets and answering questions, whilst my ears ache to hear that normal routine was resumed. The men can feel it too. Empty static buzzes as I can't answer their questions. What is happening? Where? Who is hurt? What is going on? If the incident is serious – meaning it requires outside intervention – then we would be in Standfast. They don't call it Lockdown. Daily fights, collapses and assaults on staff were quickly resolved. In Standfast, I have to stand still. Keep standing. Hold on. Hold fast and keep my shredded nerve. The men have to kept from the windows and focus on their work. It is like herding puppies, wide-eyed and worried in a pet shop, pushing their noses on the glass. Lessons have to carry on beyond their time. I am the last one standing in a room with hungry, unmedicated men. They needed their hot food and prescriptions. Standard wings rely on the canteen hatch or a kettle's burnt offerings. There are only two enhanced wings with their own cooking facilities, amounting to a toaster, microwave, and a tabletop hob. These wings are difficult to get onto and easy to be thrown off with your belongings in a few clear plastic bags. Health Care is only open twice a day for medication. Men queue for tablets, Methadone, Fentanyl, Subutex, insulin, painkillers. Each one is checked to see that they have swallowed it. Cheeking it means they can spit it out and trade it later. Plus they haven't taken their meds. Assaults and violence are doubly likely.

So here we are: hungry, hangry, and showing signs of withdrawal. I need a coffee. And after having had four children, my bladder is the size of a gnat. I really need a wee. With no hot drinks allowed in class and no going to the toilet, we are all struggling. Shifting on seats, side-eyes sliding between accomplices and Co-Ds. Sitting still for more than twenty minutes is not something they are used to. After three months in, neither am I. How do you occupy them whilst asking for permission to release them from the unit? They shouldn't see how to work the radio, and I barely know anyway. If Standfast continued, teachers would merge the classes together and take turns to keep them occupied. The men can't be left on their own or allowed to gather by the door. Fighting little fires with eight men becomes a potentially larger blaze of twenty, then thirty. English class becomes a mash-up of Barbering and Personal Development. Charades become heated.

'How is that a TV programme?'

'Kylie is a singer, not a fuckin' actress.'

'Who the hell was Genghis Khan?'

Age differences, cultural and social divides open up, quick chasms to fall into. Post-it notes don't stick on sweaty foreheads for long.

'I wanted to be Beyoncé!'

'You ain't got the arse!'

'How d'you know? Been lookin'?'

Pens are thrown across the room, followed by a chair. Picking up the chair, the pale face, now known as Adam, speaks.

'It might be better to move on to another game.'

After a quick game of musical chairs, each tatty chair shuffled, scuffled according to who thought they should have the least scruffy, smiles resume. I quickly learnt that their favourite game is hangman. Gallows humour indeed. The only time I saw men resist being escorted back to their wings for dinner was mid-game. Honour was at stake as they played in teams. Being walked back is a novelty. It means an incident is ongoing. Sometimes, it is a hostage situation. Men had barricaded the laundry room before, and it took a national Tornado squad to break the doors down after negotiations failed. By the next day, all that was left was a wet floor and complaints about dirty socks. I learnt quickly not to ask about socks, dirty or otherwise. Especially, lone socks on floors.

The state of cell floors varies from wing to wing. Unlike the Victorian tiered cellblocks with galleried landings, our prison is an old military hospital made up of two-storey buildings and prefab outbuildings. Think of a small campus university: residential blocks, gym, AstroTurf pitch, medical centre, multi-faith chapel, work areas (including kitchens and a laundry), library, gardens, education building, admin and reception buildings. Now add a segregation unit, where the most violent, troubled men are housed. A society in miniature, complete with its own prison, sprawling between high fences, watched by cameras and rooks.

There are no signs, no guide as to where to run to. No idea where you are or where you are going until you have been there a while. Just the knowledge that this is definitely no woman's land, and ideally no man's land either. Residential wings are named and have their own distinctive flavours. The Induction Wing welcomes men new into their sentence with noisy protests and induction rituals. B houses foreign nationals, and is often 'bumpy', a heady blend of world flavours. C and D are general wings, melting pots of young and old: seasoned men who know the system inside out, although less out than in; younger men, whose wide eyes belie an already thick skin. E gently holds the vulnerable prisoners. The men at the highest risk of suicide, medical crisis, assault, or mental collapse. F cradles the lifers within wooden walls, individual rooms, and a well-tended garden. G houses the enhanced men, not so much bionic as compliant and more trusted. There is an air of resilience. The pool table still has all its balls.

H and M Wings struggle to hold the men with addictions and associated difficulties. There is a small drugs rehabilitation unit connecting the two. You can smell spice from the landings, as it circles and coils the residents. For now, we'll pretend I mean paprika and not NPS, the synthetic psychoactive drug Spice. Men trying to detox share cells with dealers. Debt is rife, leading men to self-isolate behind their doors. These men were hidden from my eyes for the first year. Kind-eyed officers would tell me that those men would not be coming to class and left it at that. We would try to make sure they were not penalised. Being on basic means not being able to buy deodorant or phone calls to family. We met later, after I thought I knew what I was doing. At the beginning of the end.

I could pretend this was a familiar space, a place of learning and growth. The daily ritual helped to shape my days. I left everything behind – phone, purse, family, house, possessions. Like the men, I had no contact with the outside world. It couldn't get to me; it could get at me. No internet in the classrooms, and the twelve teachers shared one computer with limited internet access. I could reinvent myself. Begin again as a teacher proud of her origins in coal dust and potters' clay. Northern grit served me well again. I didn't make promises and always did what I said what I would. This was met with surprise and grudging trust. Men at least pretended to listen, unlike my own kids. Pale, porcelain faces cracked a smile or two. If I visited a wing, I was greeted with 'Hello's. If they yelled 'Miss', I learnt to duck or move sideways – there was trouble ahead. Then the voices in my ear. Alarm sounds. The ones I can still hear. '*Assistance required.*' Other voices in my head. 'Run.' 'Get out of the way.' 'Get out.'

I'd catch former students following me across the landings. Their gaze would rest on certain cells, nodding men inside. Walking past, the hairs on the back of my neck would tell me why. I could easily be pulled into a cell. On a wing of eighty men, there could often only be two officers present. Officers thought I was far too chirpy, always saying 'Hello' loudly as I moved along the wing spurs. It was my way of telling them where I was. Some areas had dead spots, and I didn't want to join them. The wings were a very different space to the classroom. There were some I dreaded going on, stepping over welcome mats of piss and food scraps. Others were clean and eerily silent. Never still. Just waiting. I'd hold my breath and turn up the voices. Many of the teachers refused to go on the wings at all. Strangely they were the ones who taught practical subjects. Perhaps the tension of being with men using knives and tools was their limit. It was a sign of intelligence, too. Being boundaried. Being able to separate yourself from the reality of the men's lives outside the classrooms. The wings were only a few metres away, not close enough for comfort for anyone.

Dean's nearby cell window, piled high with oranges and apples, offers cold comfort. His is the first laugh I hear each day, but he has an uncanny knack of being able to be anywhere he wants. No enclosures or doors can contain him. He has never needed a red band, the lifer's badge of honour that enables a prisoner to move around the estate unescorted. Amiable yet ethereal. All smoke and mirrors, he can get anything he wants inside. Somewhere between Fletch and Godber, he ducks and dives, wide-eyed, childlike, through hoops and under the radar.

'Kate. Did you read it?'

The scraps of paper with bold scribbled stories of his transformation sat on my desk.

'Not yet, sorry.'

'You'll like this one. Been reading Oscar again, ain't I.'

'How's the art going?'

'Was up all night just painting. Better than drugs. Did you something.'

'You really shouldn't have.'

Now I feel twinge guilty. His precious resources wasted on me again. I still hadn't read the last story he had poured onto the page, spilling his heart and guts out in sentence streams.

'No trouble. Knew you liked dragonflies, innit. It's on your desk.'

Shit. Right next to the stories that hadn't moved. Date-stamped by an old cold tea ring. And he knows we ran out of tea bags last week.

'You'd best get back. You'll miss your lunch.'

'Nah. They save me mine. Plus extra.'

Except I need him to leave. The feeling is returning to my fingers and heart. Prickled by guilt, measured by not being able to read his words. Because they bring me back to life. Lives lived and changing before my eyes. He wrote about talking to a teenager at risk, of steering a boy from danger. My protective cloak of numbness is slipping. By the time we reach the unit door, it and my mask are on the crunchy floor.

'I'll walk you back, Dean. See you safe.'

Dean laughs.

He lets me pretend. He saunters on the grass, whilst I stick to chipped concrete. We are only a few years apart in age. Our kids could be classmates. I wonder if they would be friends. Share stories. Blame prison for taking away their parents. I haven't seen my kids for a week. I think it's Thursday. Every day is the differing sameness of awkward, tiptoeing in heavy boots around what's at stake.

'Here you are.'

'That's my pad. Door always open. Fancy a brew? Got any biscuits?'

We dance around the wing entrance. Circling the gate, I dig for my keys under a chewed inhaler. They tumble out, scraping my leg to hover over my boots.

'You want to get that looked at. Let me 'ave a peek.'

A different dance begins.

'It's fine. I'm fine.'

Now the keys are caught inside the chain links, locked in an embrace. I struggle. He moves back, seeing someone pushing their hands through the bars.

Once free, I unlock the wing and haul the iron gate back.

'Gentlemen first.'

'I ain't no gent, Kate.'

'And I'm no lady. That's Dr Kate to you.'

We snigger. His eyes squint, and I turn away to bang the gate back into its frame. Lock it. Bump my hip against it to check. Then my arse glides past it again. Thank God for love handles.

We dance the same routine again with a spectator caught between the main gate and the unit barrier.

'Let me in, Miss.'

'I'm sorry. I can't. I'll get an officer to come over.'

I have to unlock the next gate and get Dean past me without letting the other man past as well. Then I have to lock the gate without allowing the other man through or near my keys. This isn't my welcoming classroom. We are not on familiar ground now. It sucks my breath out into the heavy air. Common courtesy has gone. I push past him and lock the gate between us.

Dean has already taken possession of a plastic tray piled high with potatoes, beans pooling over the sides.

Tell me. Do you hear the squeaking breathing behind you?

Am I still in character? Do you see how uncomfortable I feel?
Can you see the flashbacks across my eyes? Can you see them
pushing past? Pushing me in? Can you hear the screams? The
alarms? The silence after? The cover-up?

'That looks eeerm . . . nice. I'd best be getting back.'

'Alright, Kate. See ya tomorra. Safe.'

I leave him gulping down his dinner. I tell myself that he is
on his own because he is late. I shouldn't be here. I shouldn't
have come back. Later, I will creep into my house, clutching
shoes. My throat is burning, secrets scratching to get out.

After a week of teaching this class spelling through photos of
dodgy tattoos, report writing, with articles on new technology,
and calming heated discussions on the possibility of future
employment, I am ready to leave it all behind for a weekend of
quiet white noise screaming in my ears. I have been battling
to understand the system for arranging support once a man
leaves prison. My student is facing homelessness in a few
weeks. He has been refused a hostel place and is trying to
contact family. We set a time to work through his options after
the weekend. I thought I was championing the underdog.
I made the mistake of making some enquiries at the end of
the day. I got my fingers burnt there. It turns out my gentle,
green-eyed, non-smoking learner was an arsonist – which
means he cannot be given certain types of accommodation.
And his family won't be able to help. Let's just say he burnt his

bridges there already. But Saturday beckons. Time to sleep, catch up on the washing, and remember all the people I left outside. Remember who I am on the outside. The airlock breathes a sigh of relief as I leave. Even the air beyond the fences smells different. Spore-laden, dusty white clouds were forming behind me. Red-eyed and allergic to pollen, I drive home with Dean's first attempt at watercolour pooled on the passenger seat, lucky that for once I don't have to hide my messy thoughts from John.

The one night I actually made it to bed, I have a violent awakening. Shocked awake by screams from outside the room. These aren't in my head.

'Mum, where is it you work again?'

'Why? I am trying to have a lie-in . . .'

'Because it's on TV. It's on fire.'

Stomach lurches forward as I cough up imagined smoke. There it is. Yellow flames racing through the roof of a wing. Smoke billowing for miles. I struggle to breathe. There are over ninety men in there. And staff. Friends. Students. People. All locked within a unit. Within cells. Jesus. Choked for words. Not for the first time, thoughts of those men, tired and vulnerable, come to my door. Now they are in front of my eyes. I watch the news report each time it appeared, shortening and progressively condensed into a five-minute segment by the evening news. I still can't speak, other than murmurs of despair and hope. My worlds have collided in my living room, and the kids have quickly lost interest. They have moved onto other things found on phones, swiping away the dangerous reality of prisons at the touch of a screen. As their hands conduct a virtual orchestra, I hold onto my chair. I reason with my whirling thoughts. I can smell smoke. Plumes of fear rising and curling round my throat.

I stutter and judder back to reason. I choke on the sweet fumes from Dean's fruit-filled cell. I cough through the night: panicked Code Blue asthma. No call for assistance available here. No response. Lynne messages me to ask if I have to go back, eager for gossip and talking about how I don't belong there anyway. She doesn't know why I teach people she calls criminals: it is a waste of time. She launches into her standard rant about how prisons are way better than care homes. I have long since given up trying to persuade her. Perhaps, if I had fifty years of gradually dripping lies into her eyes like the press had, I would stand a chance. We've talked about this. About blood on the floors, flooded cold showers, eating by a toilet, shitting in front of your cellmate, meds given only twice a day, paying twice as much for a limited TV service and extortionate amounts for short phone calls. Most men who have a phone stashed away in a wall or light fitting only use it to call home. Some do use phones to order drugs and contraband. Or to video incidents. And I begin to smile as I realise that the video footage the BBC news is using was not filmed from a nearby farmhouse, as they claimed. The angles are all wrong. It was recorded inside the fences, from the Induction Wing, which I walk past every morning. And the wing on fire is next to Education. I can hear Dean's words and thoughts from the discomfort of my home.

I can hear lads yelling. Proper loud. Am already awake after some dickhead tripped the electric so all the fuckin' alarm bells went off. They ain't getting any quieter. Summat's up. They're getting proper aggy. Gone on way longer than a scrap. Would've been knocked out way before now.

That ain't vape or tea bags I can smell, either. Keys are jangling loud. Boots coming on the landing. They know better than that here. Summat's wrong.

The door bangs open.

'Up! Get up. Move out. We're moving out. Leave your stuff. Now!'

'What's happening?'

'We need you all out.'

'Too fuckin' right. Let's get going, then.'

Frogmarched in me bare feet. Hairy bear feet. We're in a line. Like a fuckin' chain gang. But ain't no one singin'. I know where I am. We head to the gym. I sneak a look back. My stuff better be safe. My whole world is in there. I've grabbed me photo, screwed it in me shorts. They ain't getting that. But all me books, me work. Going up in flames again. This time for real. It's glowing like a fuckin' vape coil. Orange, yellow, white streaks, like devils leaving the building. Well, this is my hell. Set free at night and squashed into the gym. Sweating more than ever. I ain't the only one. Will they search the place? Find all them things I don't want them to. Feel sorry for the other lads. Some well dodgy stuff stashed they think I don't know about. But I ain't into that anymore. That game's for mugs. I could murder a smoke, though.

Over the long hours, a trickle of rumours began to douse my own worst fears. The fire had been brought under control during the night. Everyone had got out alive and been sent to the gym hall. In the face of what must be their worst nightmare, the staff were the heroes and heroines of the hour. Switching from calm bed checks and welfare visits to a full-scale evacuation of over ninety grumpy, half-awake, or scared men, the night staff were nothing short of incredible. Typical of prison staff, though, to value all human life. No throwing away the keys there. Night staff were often waiting by the gate to be let out, grinning like naughty school kids bunking off school before it started. Never thanked, prison staff keep our fears from us and ask nothing in return. They also live hidden lives behind closed gates. Wide, large windows afford them no privacy in office spaces. Sightlines work both ways. Always watched, searched for secrets. Knowledge is currency whichever side of the law you stand on.

Monday morning came slowly. Black roof trusses punctured the sunrise, dark ribs spread open. Smoke breath had already left the burnt body. It was hard to ignore. A makeshift fence surrounded the wing until a tall steel fence was built long months later. Until then, men circled the body, watching for weaknesses. Men were found on the roof, causing lockdowns. More regular fights in the grounds distracted from men sneaking into the wing to steal stashed drugs and phones. All the residents had been shipped out in what they were wearing, their few possessions left behind in the stricken pirate ship. Stories of meds hoards, food parcels, and contraband lay heavy in the asbestos-laden air. Men spoke of personal photos lost not to the flames, but to the asbestos-tainted water that followed. Washed away tears for scanned pictures and chalk drawings. Some of the men returned to the prison. The cheery-faced loveable rogue greeted me with a wolf whistle before I arrived at the unit door. That small sound alone could get him extra days inside. The mercurial Dean slipped back through the cracks, a silver sliver along the path edges he rushed over to say 'Hello', heart and eyes wide open.

Dean once again became a regular in the education building. His laugh could be heard well before he entered the corridor. He still had an affable knack of being able to move around the estate unfettered, string bag slung across his back, no accompanying officer. His paintings in bright, garish colours matured and darkened after he came back to us. He spoke, ashen-faced, of phoenixes rising from the flames. Serving seven years, I knew he was possibly more than a dealer and less than a murderer. But I didn't ask and he never said. We stayed in the present. The now and here, we were. Back in prison together. Some days I taught him about spelling and art history or how to structure a story. Most days he taught me about how to live in the alternative reality of prison. Where the little things mattered. A smile went far, but a look went too far. Where everything – people, objects, words – had two sides.

Prison language was ever-changing, even if some kept to their former roles. Drug dealers were always food farmers, but their crops were rotated between colours, letters, objects, and playing cards in cell viewing panels. Always one step ahead. The words here will already be out of date. Words were made up and flitted between gangs inside and outside. Piff and peng batted over nets and fences like the tennis balls full of drugs. Of course, court was a forbidden word. Yet men were adept at holding court, performing their egos to an audience to inflate their position or mask a darker side. Those masks fell when I saw their records. From easy-going lad to child-rapist in the click of a mouse. Stumbling, quiet family man to sex-trafficker. Glazed photos of addicts were unrecognisable in the faces of clear-eyed men with an air of knowledge I saw in lessons. I witnessed a few falls from grace, equal to that of an Oedipus or Othello. Pride came before each fall, as pushing Iagos sat on many an angel's wing.

I put on a brave face when going into a new class of the unknown. I deliberately wore a pink or flowery dress. Few would hit a woman, but I seemed to meet most of them. Some would kill one, though, and I met those with blind, blissful ignorance until nods and side-eyes alerted me to the assumed dangerous past that might spill into the present. Each class was a performance. They began with nervous preparation, learning lines, and tingling fingers, awaiting the rest of the cast. Taking turns to be the star turn and the audience, lessons were more devised and improvised than I cared to admit to my managers. There was a set course outline and lesson plans for every level of student. But there were some days in which the sole aim was to not go down in flames. Where the objective was that everyone made it out alive.

In the shadow of the skeleton wing, the routine breaks ranks and staples another moment in the scrapbook. I am unusually anxious. Even more anxious than my normal level. I'd raised that bar already. Nothing seems to be staying in its place. Something is shifting underfoot. I pull up my sleeves. Splashes of teal, blue, and purple bleed out over the lines scored into my arm. The outline of a dragonfly lies still, captured in my skin before it could take flight. Grounded and wide-eyed, we begin. There's a weight to the air, prickling and anxious. Something big has definitely happened. The next few hours will tell if it is close by or on the out. For now, it hovers.

When they return to class, it's clear we need to talk.

'Miss. That tower. I knew people. That's my street right there.'

We sit for a moment, silently. For once, I have no words.

Hourly minutes pass until I suggest a choice between looking at the papers and another exercise. Here they have a choice between that hard place and a rock of educational material.

'Can we see what they've said, Miss?'

Papers rustle open, slide shared across the room, and heads hang. Eyes fixed on the black cage of a burnt-out tower block. Grenfell. Empty-windowed eyes fixed and dilated. No movement. Flatlined lips twitch and flicker to life.

'Miss. They left us to burn.'

'No. The firefighters asked people to stay inside their flats because they should have been safe. It's standard procedure to stop crowding on the stairwells. They didn't know that the cladding wasn't safe.' I struggle to defend those put in the firing line.

'No. They put us in a thirty-whatever-storey box and watched us go up. Look at it. We had no chance. That's how it is.'

The boisterous voices of yesterday murmured their pain. A palpable ache present in the room. Eyes closed, shutters down as heads rocked in quiet, bowed unison. Embodied grief and empathy in a room several hundred miles away from the angry core of smouldering ashes. In a classroom next to a burnt-out wing. A wing several of them were in when it went up.

'Man knows people there. My people.'

'Our people.'

'True dat.'

'Ain't no one being done for that. Too many riches blocking out the light.'

Long, slow exhale. Aching head and heart. Tight ribs are

beginning to close. Weight of knowing struggles to surface above the tingling hands. Sad panic is beginning to rise through arms to flicker across chests and necks. We need to breathe again.

'What would you like to do? How can I show you that I am listening?'

That I can't imagine coming from a place where injustice and corruption are normalised and expected? Either here or there. How do we begin to shake the weight of silence off? Can we rise up and be counted, be seen above the tragedy tourists crowding the site to leave words of sorrow? How can we write the words lying under the skin?

'Can we do something?'

'Send things to help?'

'What do you think would be useful?'

'Toothbrushes, food, blankets, all that.'

'Let's do it.'

By the end of the week a set of decorated murky green crates leaves the airlock gates. As the door slides back, the sound of exhaled air sighs into the birdsong outside. Decorated with stars and words of hope by Dean. The boxes gave him a chance to reflect on their own collective moment of trauma. Of being dragged from their beds and left with nothing. Of the fear and panic they still feel when they hear a fire alarm. Eyes darting side to side. Instant meerkats. They know what lay behind and ahead for the survivors. For those who had little and lost everything, the Grenfell boxes join a van bound for

London. Inside the tins of food, towels, and colouring books lies a thread of connection. Breadcrumbs from the lost sons back to their point of origin. Veins and arterial highways hold each other close.

3.

Monday was greeted by the usual fragrance of L'Eau de Greggs mixed with regret and insomnia. Wet haired and wired eyed, I walk in on autopilot. Second nature means I can be more prepared for the little surprises. The added toppings of violence, collapse, and threats, which the day might sprinkle on my shit sandwich. Into each life a little rain must fall. But in class, it was pouring in through the ceiling tiles. Observations, assessments, results, reports, exam preparation, invigilation. All extra. Never enough to get a good pass rate or support men through their first sustained experience of lessons. Getting them housing after release. Sorting proper diagnoses for medical conditions. Supporting a man with dementia, who forgets another line from his favourite poem each week. Working on the wings, despite its dangers and immediacy, was beginning to feel like a serious possibility.

For now, the classroom awaits. Half covered in posters and student work, and half blank to avoid triggering the ADHD students. A game of two halves. Neither winning. No score draw this week, so far. Bag dumped in locker. Coffee slurped on the move.

'*Assistance required in Health Care.*'

That's an extra few minutes of preparation time. The yelling outside stops and the man huffs and puffs back to his wing. All my paperwork is hidden from view. The comments on support needed (pages), current progress (lines), educational history (words). The day's work is already on the tables. It's all to play for. Set seats to keep eyelines straight. I'm not so concerned about a path between me and the door. I've known this lot for three weeks now. Trust has been earned both ways. We are now in the run up to exams. Time to work on exam anxiety. Mainly mine. We remove all traces of where they are studying. Because some believe they shouldn't have the chance to begin again. Even the ones who have barely started out. Today they will mark each other's work. Pride and status are put aside in the margins. My fingers are tingling with the first sparks of nerves for the day. For this day. Every day. I shuffle papers and count the pens going onto tables. Class lists at the ready.

I register someone walking towards me.

My boss. Unusual to see him this the other side of the door, not screened off by report spreadsheets.

His walk is different. Not the swagger of an observer. Not the stride of a guide showing off his well-controlled domain. He has a right to be proud. We are doing well given what we have to work with: haphazard regimes, twice-daily incidents, shifting population. The men are not the issue. But this is not the movement of a happy man. He is furrowed. Lines around young eyes.

'Kate. There's a phone call for you.'

'But I am about to teach.'

'Lock up. Come into the office. You can take it there.'

I fit the key in the lock and force it round. Follow him to the end of the corridor. Men are starting to arrive.

He waits by his office door; the deputy manager stands beside him. I can taste the air. Chewy and bitter.

As I pick up the phone, I realise. This can't be good. It's not going to be a mother calling in to ask if I can ring a prison in Manchester to tell them her son has already passed his exams. You'd think this was the one teaching job without helicopter parents. He is kicking-off and is in isolation until they can calm him. Once is enough.

This is quieter. An almost unfamiliar voice. My husband. Soft spoken strength. He doesn't belong here.

'Are you sitting down?'

'Am now.'

'The police have been to see your brother.'

'OK.'

'It's your dad.'

Silence.

'He's been found dead.'

'OK.'

'You need to go up there.'

'OK.'

'Take care. Drive safe. Just get back.'

I put the phone down. And cradle my head for a second or two. The door has been open all the time. Still, they wait outside.

'I need to go.'

'It's fine. We've already cancelled your class. Are you OK to drive?'

'Not yet. I'll gather my things.'

My thoughts. My heart. My lungs. My legs and my hands are shaking.

Time to straighten up and wobble into the staffroom. Dean is already there. Pretending to clean the sink as he completes another coffee round, always including himself. Larger than life shrinks as I enter. Deflated with all the bravado air let out. He recognises the look. Loss walked in.

'You OK? Stupid question that, eh? Have a coffee. Put sugar in, like. Even as I know you don't have it, normal.'

Nothing is normal now. The last part of where I am from has gone. Hearing the gentle calm words where he is not allowed to be for fear of contamination. Trauma tales cannot be unheard. Yet there he was. Telling of leaving. More safety lines severed. Bloodlines cut. Places now without reasons to return.

I'm a forty-six-year-old orphan. Sliding. Falling. He catches me in his eyes and we sit down.

'Was he old and that? Have another coffee. You going to drive? Sit here for a bit longer, like.'

I have nothing to offer in between his questions. He holds

me in his wide heart. He's never mentioned his own dad. Neither have a place here. I don't even know if he has a dad. And he shouldn't have to carry the loss of mine.

I get up to take the coffee and then find myself sat down again. We sit for silent minutes while he chews his lips.

'You OK? Don't go till you have to. Leave it a bit.'

He stands. Then he puts down his precious string netting bag. The one normally held so skin cutting close. It's left on the chair opposite. And he sits down. No laughter. No booming voice echoing empty platitudes. He just sits down. Beside me. Because he knows there are no words.

We say nothing. Holding cups close. Fingers meeting round the sides. Steamy coffee trails mask the skin shimmer sweat. But I am cold. Stopped, stalled, still, whilst the clamour of classroom arrivals carries on regardless. A loud yell of joy as one of my errant learners leaves the building without either of us being subjected to a daily dose of grammar and the best Anglo-Saxon language.

'I'd better get going.'

Getting up is easier. Sea legs have washed away. Shored up by a temporary resolve to move. I need to move. I'm caught between worlds. Clutching my bag and coat, I leave him behind. He'll leave me later, too.

'Drive safe.'

His face empties further as I leave the unit and lock it behind the door. Another reminder of the divides that should keep us apart. He is standing upright, face fallen. There's nothing more he can do. The door sighs shut with relief, releasing the trapped space between.

She is falling. I am looking at a proper nosedive. Going down crash like a kamikaze. Seen that look before. See it again likely soon. Lads lost a mate, girlfriend, mum, last subby. I have tried to be kind before and they have taken the piss. Called me a mug. But I don't care because I know who I am. I am who I was supposed to be from the beginning. I am reborn, but the other one is still there if I need him. Ready to rise and cause mayhem if they back me into a corner. I am on a mission to be kind. Love conquers hate. I will stick with the ones who have shown me what it is like to have friends who don't want anything in return. The ones who put me on a better path. Guardian angels put the devil away. They saved me from the other ways: the drugs, the mess, the scraps, the aggy. The people who take and take without giving. Don't get it twisted. I can spot them miles off now. It would be easy to go back. But nothing good is easy. Easy is for losers. Not for me. Not no more. No more mayhem for me or them. Stopped all that game. There are bigger things to do with my time. One day I will go through that door without having to smile it unlocked. I will take my books and paint my way out like a phoenix rising from the flames. I have done it before and I will do it again. This time it will be for good. No messing. No point. I'm done with all that. Got new things to think about. Stuff to read, paint, do, build. I'm all for fixing up me. No time for stopping. Best keep going. Keep strong.

Driving to meet in the middle, the other newborn orphan greets me. Let's go home. To find out what remains. Greeted by a boarded door and glass-showered pathway. Just like work. But our keys are useless now. I joke that I should have brought a student with me. We break in through the back door. Exchange looks. We have nothing. Know nothing. How long ago. Where. Why. The house creaks, straining under the weight of the hoarded tins and rubbish. It wants to stop. It doesn't need to protect him anymore. Now in control, it wants to fall in. Close the cracked walls and drop the weight of loss.

I'm lost until I see the husks of incomplete puzzles, unread papers, half-built lawnmower in the kitchen. We're all left unfinished.

I have two weeks' compassionate leave. It doesn't help. I flit between rooms stuffed with everything from the time before. When she died, we'd been able to clear the layers of hoarded food, papers, materials, broken TVs. She could always make something out of nothing. The yellow slice of clinical waste bags sneaked back from hospital were the worst. Locked away inside made it easier. I stayed in my empty rooms whilst he drowned in memories. Tending to the dead whilst I fought for the living.

Now it was different. And the same. Watch, wedding ring, and wallet laid out on the table by the chair he never woke up from. Emptiness and order amidst the chaos. So different from the empty cells I had left behind. This one was padded with the past, boxes of photos and telegrams jostling for position with mouse-filled packs of toilet roll. Those were gold-dust currency inside. Corn in Egypt. No future here.

Pipped to the post by a heart attack. The last post stuck to the porch floor. Like the three men that year so far, he hadn't woken up. Uniforms surged in and tried to bring him back. Blue lights. Always sirens. Is this how victims feel? Stillness whilst everything whirls around the room. Carries on as normal. Loud conversations. People hustling. Traffic outside. School runs and work runs. The work that doesn't love you back. Too busy to notice what has happened. To us. No respect. Last week I'd sat by a pale face when he became the head of the family. His image sits with me now. Across the kitchen table covered with well-meaning teacups. A mad teacher's tea party. I stare at mine. Tea bags hide the future. Clean slate. We can begin to reinvent and forget. Don't speak ill of the dead. As if I would. Why is it easier to be kind to strangers? Not to the man who worked in a job he hated to keep stale bread and broken biscuits on the table. This table. A Formica nightmare in skip-broken blue.

As we begin to empty the house, draining it of our bloodlines, I fill my head with work. Going into the stripped-back isolation cells brings cold comfort. No signs of family, no memories held in the walls. Here are new stories. Immediate. Raw red-written in lines across arms and thighs. Something tangible and worthwhile. Someone alive. Human.

The meaning of life is here. In the whitewashed walls and bare copper pipes. Water, food, a place to sleep. A rare place where the disconnected can begin to think. In pieces, yelling, and banging the walls behind the library. Or quietly curled in a single blue cellular blanket. Childhood comforts. Watched over. Kept safe. Away from harm. But wherever you go, you take yourself. There's no escaping them. The voices of regret, hope and despair. The ones lost and the ones to come.

'Eh, Kate! You're back! Good to see you.'

'And you.' I can feel the blood coming back into my veins. Flowing and surging again. 'How've you been?'

'You know. But that's life, innit. Another story for you on your desk.'

'I look forward to it. What are you up to today?'

'Putting up posters. Gets me out and about. You seen the fence yet?'

'Which one? Why? Have you been busy?'

'Done some graffiti. Proper covered it. Lads and I took ages. Could have taken longer but they only had a day. Keep adding rats round the back, though. Can't keep me in, can they?'

'See you later, Dean.'

'Yeah. Safe.'

Except she ain't safe. She's still got that look. Keepin' busy. Too busy. Still, keeps me up. Gives me things to do. Pictures to paint. Devils dancing. Bosch skinny devils. Given me my tag now.

They are amazing. What a look. Can see 'em in me sleep. When I do sleep. Dream and think about what will be. Once the wild walls have gone, I'll paint ladders, tunnels, ratholes through to the other side. When I am back home. I will keep making my stars. I will keep lifting spirits and spreading rainbows, rising. I am strong enough to carry them. A tiger hiding behind a dragon. I will keep getting stronger and find my way.

Whilst he scurries around the edges, I go onto the wing even Dean's mercurial skills cannot find a way into. I need a more intense distraction from the swirling thoughts. Segregation was the only place I had never seen Dean. The one place he didn't want to go. With just cause. The smell of disinfectant was a welcome awakening. Eye-prickling work took me away from the weight of bloodlines. I was slowly being buried alive. Becoming burnt out. Looking at pale cigarette skin circles and living stories that I recognised. Painful awakenings with razors. Through the looking glass we went. All we were allowed were felt tip pens and single sheets of paper. Broken plastic did less damage than a metal Biro. Writing tangled memories of objects, places, and people whilst swinging our legs over the edge of the metal bed. Holding pain in metaphors. Pages of paper skin stories. Imagined and real queued up in lines of ill-fated doubt. Those stories I held safe within. Shared, then shut away. Storing up trouble for later.

Unlocking my classroom again, things have moved.

Everything is shifting. Pens and books have gone. Dictionaries stolen. The most valuable ones: the foreign language ones translating despairing cries in Somali or raging torrents of Polish. These were locked behind more doors than most. Whoever took them had keys. Thieves with keys. For fuck's sake. I try to imagine that staff needed to borrow them to support vulnerable men. With the steady tide of men in need, the books never found their way back. Lost at sea. Washed up on foreign shores.

With those books, Ardo learnt to write his name and a basic email. It took ten weeks before he stopped smiling. In fractured words, he told me he was being deported.

'This letter.'

'Would you like me to read it for you?'

'No. They send me back.'

'How long have you lived here?'

'Twelf year.'

'So most of your life.'

'Mother gone. To market. Not come back. Same many.'

'How did you cope? Do you have other family?'

'Father he die. Army. Sister gone. Then she send for me. Tell me things. Mother. With bad men. Sold. Sister she send for all of us.'

This wide-eyed, smiling parcel of humanity. Without parents or homeland. Meeting my eyes with his. Sent from place to place. I didn't like sending him back to the wing. Swallowed him whole. Washed down by a tide of grey, rougher men, who were often found shaking his hand, whispers shifting to loud laughter when an officer walked past.

A week later he was ghosted. Taken during the night without warning. Jail bird forcibly flown home. He still sits at the back of the class in my head, alongside the ones I have tried to hold on to. Still in relative safety, I can keep the grey wolves from him and follow him back to the wing on canteen days. Ardo was even awarded one of Dean's prestigious gold stars. It became a point of honour to be given a skimpy, thin yellow paper star from Dean. They were handmade, bright words of encouragement, now folded inside a book I can't open yet. They were Dean's attempt to bring cheer and positive reinforcement to a world where rehabilitation got lost along the way. Where nothing stayed the same and every day was different. Meaningful change was distracted by moments of danger and risk. Movement meant the men were on their way across the estate. Coming to a standstill in class. A pause before action. Learning not to be active. To sit with yourself and work out who that was. And who you wanted it to be. But then it was easy to get distracted. You had to notice everything. Have eyes in your arse, as my grandma would say.

My arse is always well covered. Leggings and a dress. Knees and shoulders covered. Not sure why shoulders are such an issue. There is normally a reason. One you can't unhear. No coffee or other hot drinks in class after a teacher was kettled. Fingers burnt and face blistered after an ill-advised comment. The level below sugaring though. A sweet revenge where sugar is mixed with the water to make it stick to the skin. No squirming out of that so quickly. It is hard to judge how men might react. The goalposts change every four or six weeks. A new morning class each month. A not-so-fresh-faced afternoon class every six weeks. This is the entry-level class. Only entry-level in education's eyes. Hardened, narrow graduate eyes reign over the odd wide-eyed newbie to the system. Eyes roll out and hide in the corners of the class. Amongst the dirt and dust. I have to scoop them back in quickly. How can there be people here who cannot read or write? Everything you say will be taken down in evidence against you. Failure to disclose something now will also be used against you.

'Nice tattoo, Miss.'

'For someone?'

It hovers unsaid. We all know what it means. Silence holds the impossibility of words to describe what grief is.

'We ain't doin' Shakespeare, are we?'

''Cause it 'ain't proper English.'

'Actually, it's funny you should say that, but . . .'

'No, Miss, we ain't up to that.'

'Hang on a minute.'

Clinging to the edges of the paper. Just look. Take a minute. See how the words rise and fall, persuading you to listen and see.

'No way, Miss. I mean we like you an' all, but we ain't doin' that. I told you. We ain't needin' that on road.'

'So let's play bingo.'

'Now you're talking. What do we win?'

'My undying attention.'

'We got that already. Where's the sweets?'

Still in Tesco. In the aisle of processed foods, ready meals, and last-minute squashed cakes for school fayres. The aisle invisibly marked 'Teacher's Essentials'. The one visited late at night once the heavy belt and chain have been wound off. Could you imagine the *Daily Mail* headlines if I brought them in?

'Fair enough, Miss. Can we get on with it, then?'

As if I haven't been trying for the last ten minutes. This is meant to be where I am in control. Away from the bickering relatives and scavengers. Paper recourse of definitions, score cards, and three extracts flutters round the room to land in front of each face.

'So who do you think will have the highest number of persuasive language features: Trump, Martin Luther King, or Shakespeare?'

''Kin easy, Miss. My man Shakespeare.'

'So let's see, shall we?'

'I ain't readin' the long bit. I'll do this one. "Tomorrow and tomorrow and tomorrow". Goes on a bit, doesn't he? Proper chewin'. Bare fed up. As if there might not be a tomorrow. But if man leaves shanks behind, then there ain't no tomorrow. Self-defence. Out like a candle. Snuffed.'

'My mate had bare candles on the street. And flowers. Couldn't see the pavement. Proper cover-up.'

'You do realise you've just read Shakespeare and understood it? And reflected on how universal the words are?'

'Miss, you tricked me. Isit?'

'That ain't fair. Serious though? Isit?'

'So you can read poetry. And human drama.'

'You kidding, Miss. I am livin' the drama. Every day. Livin' the dream.'

'Nah, you are the drama. You is active.'

'Do you know what that is, Miss?'

'Yes, I do. Let's keep to the plan. My plan, not yours.'

'As soon as you know the words, we change 'em. Keep it fresh. Keep ahead. Like patois, but quicker. Streets stay ahead of the feds. And you, Miss.'

'I don't doubt it. But that's what Shakespeare did, too. Made up words. Stayed south of the river to avoid the eyes of the law. Lived hand-to-mouth on the edge of respectability.'

'We ain't no poets.'

But look at you. Look at your arms and shoulders. Walking poems armed with words, shouldering the weight of the lost. Names scored across your back bearing witness to feuds and a modern revenge tragedy still in motion. You can't look back without mirrors. Propelled into a drama of politics and the harm done to each other in the name of another justice. Just stop. Look. Tell me. Don't show me. Don't move. Don't act out revenge. Speak of it. Speak as one who has gone before. Speak to those who might come after. Break down if you have to. Break the circle of trust. Break the cycle. Swirling circles of script around names of belonging. Permanent but only skin deep. Poetry in motion.

You are waking walking words and living stories. How are you going to end the story? What genre are you going to choose? Is there a choice? We talk about making better choices, but what exactly are your options? Which plots are available to you? Tragedy? Thriller? Comedy? And will you be the hero, or the villain? Will you bare your soul so that others might see? Might just glimpse the poetry of your life? The suffering for your art?

'Rap. Now you're talkin', though.'

'Drill scene. Bare money now.'

'Doesn't it incite violence, though? Isn't that why the government are trying to get it removed from YouTube?'

Words fire back and forth. Colours Green and directions East square up and flutter down. Bonded blood brothers smirk and swagger, swaying in the breeze of murmured memories.

As we are about to land on the shore, safely perched on shifting sands, the end of the session is called.

'*Release from Labour and Education.*'

'Not too bad today, Miss. Maybe more Trump, though. He is going to cause some violence.'

They take aim and lift off through the door that barely hangs onto its hinges.

4.

'And that's how you blow up a cash machine, Miss.'

'I'll bear that in mind if the whole teaching thing doesn't work out, but I doubt I could get all that kit in my handbag.'

'Don't be fuckin' daft. You can buy two Dolce ones with all that cash. And pay someone to carry 'em for you. Fourteen K min.'

As the music from the barbering class radio drifts up the stairwell, my thoughts spiral down to meet the chemicals it sits next to on the shelf. Here's one student who could name every chemical compound for the exam. God help us if he finds his way into that Aladdin's cave. Luckily most of his components are missing. Outside, where all the connections and binding agents hid in plain sight.

The other learners are slow to arrive. Making the most of the sunshine between wings, fit flitting between dark brick stripes. You'd think they would all be escorted in at the same time. But there could be twenty minutes between the first and last. A useful time for talk, never small. Glimpses of nights spent blocking out the screaming drug dreams of a neighbour. Of dread at being released in a few weeks. Of families, cars, homes, and all that has been left behind. All the things that have been taken. All the things that have been stolen. By them or from them. Being given time meant losing connections. They say you can't buy time, but here you can at a heavy price. Further short stories of extra days added for being caught with a phone. For dealing. For not saying anything at all. For speaking out.

'Miss. I need to speak to yer. Now. Not in a fuckin' minute. Reet now. I don't need no fuckin' English. I am not fuckin' comin' in. I'm telling yer. I'm not fuckin' doin' it! You'll not get me through that fuckin' door. I do not want to be 'ere.'

I can feel his anger and the faint sweat smell of Fray Bentos. Toe-touching sheer fury staring at me. Spittle peppers my eyes. The mouth of hell has opened up. Until I stare back. Step back. And tell him that I don't want him, either, in that mood. This is not the distraction I was hoping for. The Manchester lilt is pulling like a single-hair-strained ponytail. Sharp. To the core. Under my skin and back home. The place of half-emptied, abandoned houses.

'That makes two of us, then. But they will take away your TV – which you pay for – and your pay until you come back. And they will keep putting you on my register and interrogate me about your absence. It's all about the asses on seats and the retention, apparently. So let's just get this done. Man – and woman – up.'

'Shite. That accent. You Northern?'

'Not quite in some eyes. Your point?'

'Shite. Don't mess wi't fellow Northerner. Especially a lass. Manchester, right? Where should I sit?'

'What's your name?'

'A1234AA'

'No, your name. You're not a number. We share names here. I'm Kate.'

'Alreet, Miss.'

Sigh.

'Today, we're starting off with spelling.'

Groans and two pens already skate across the table, freed from any further work.

'Don't matter no more.'

'Got autocorrect on me phone.'

Sniggers.

'And you've never caused a ruck because it changed a word?'

Silence.

'Well, there was that one time . . .'

'I don't mean duck. Never.'

'Where I'm from, it's a term of endearment.'

'Like cock?'

And we're off again. This time it's laughter. Swear words mistaken. Added and taken away. Meanings and Ofsted regulations fly out of the window. After squelching against the grubby pane and sliding down to the slim gap between rotten frames.

There are tough crowds and then there's this class.

Alternating between savvy, sassy quips and silence. Loaded comments, goading gang tags and open invitations. They could teach the Royal Shakespeare Company about sightlines. No matter how many times their seats were re-configured, owlnecks linked looks and the promise of later-settled debts. Two rival gangs in one small room.

The big not-so-smart screen flickers, taking full charge of the situation. Look at me. Not at each other. Forget the scores held back in the wings. Leave prison theatre for a while. This is an intermission. A display of other disastrous bodies to consider. To watch. Time to disengage contact. To be curious about what the body can say without speaking. What stories it can tell about class, and pain, and the past. And, rather sneakily, spelling.

One by one, the uncanny stories emerge. Breaking through the misspelt tattoo images, words are both reclaimed and reordered.

'"To young to die, to fast to live" – what's wrong with that, Miss?'

Where do we start? On the streets where you grew up in a gang promising family ties and blood bonds? The speed at which you've listed the friends lost to knives, cars, bullets. Perhaps we should stick to the words. Rewrite the story into one of privilege and education. Of Latin homophones, which are interchanged to correct. Correction. Another difficult word to think about. To change the mistake. To rewrite. Or are they already written off?

'"No Ragrets" – oh my days! That's bad! What's with people?!

That's going to take some cover-up.'

Perhaps a row of wildflowers, roses, or skulls. Botanical prints betray the heart of another. But like it or not, even though we shouldn't judge a book by its cover, we do look at the words. And now I'd change that lesson and reframe it outside the realms of tattoo shaming. I'm still learning. Those tell of leaving school too early, both artist and muse conspiring to show the body's origins. Place, accent, and lack of access to education. Stolen privilege. You can't afford a decent brief. Be brief. To the point. Unlike your sentence. Now a celebration of words, a need to write, speak silently to others. To speak out of the inside and connect.

'Miss, looking at bad tattoos was OK, I guess.'

'Can we do letters next? I need to write home.'

'I need to sort my appeal.' Winking. 'A different kind of cover-up.'

'Gotta make it look good.'

'Them language things we did. Every little helps. My baby mom ain't happy with the lack of money. Funny how she didn't mind when the money was comin' in. Where did she think it came from, the fuckin' tooth fairy?'

'To be fair, mate, you missing a few.'

'That's not the only thing he missing. Congratulate him, Miss. He be a dad again soon. I hear his missus is five months gone and he's been in for a year.'

And we're off again. Round eight, or it is nine? I've lost count and there's no bell to save us. Simmer down and slimmer down.

Shrink back the puffed-out chests and squared-up shoulders. Sit down and have a look at this newspaper. Big headlines, lurid pictures, and we're back in the room reading about other worlds. Places where objects and things matter so much more. Where colours are seen, not felt or heard. I hear colours, and they feel the Code Yellow on B Wing. Frantic bat ears pick up on the alarm in my ear.

'Where's that, Miss?'

'Your pad?'

'Nah, your lot ain't active this week.'

'Alright there.'

'Safe.'

'Say nothing.'

Fist bump.

'Say nothing.'

'Safe.'

They squash their noses against the windows, a reminder of stolen childish days past. We have the biggest windows on the estate. A scurry of black and white runs ahead. There's always one who doesn't hurry, visibly hoping it will be all over by the time they arrive. And so we try not to watch. A band of grey lead by a purposefully bright pink dress drifts into no-man's-land.

'We can go now, can't we? I missed lunch yesterday and by the time I got back it was bang up. That ain't happening again. No chance. It's canteen today, too.'

'Have another quiz sheet.'

Look at another vain attempt to keep you all occupied and contained. No one can leave the building yet.

'Miss, I'm off.' He scrapes his chair across the floor and pushes the table away. 'You can't stop me. It's gone time.'

'So, here's the thing . . .'

The elephant in the room who is now cowering in the corner, watching, and waiting for how we are going to get out of this one.

'We need to stay right here. I can't let you leave.'

We can all see the man on the charred roof next door. Waving his arms like he is on a motorway bridge. Except no one is passing by. No one can go in and get him, either, because he is on the broken trusses of an unsafe building full of melted asbestos. For an instant I want to truss him up like a yo-yo and lower him onto the ground. The disruption causes a standfast. Again. But I suspect the culprit has been dared to do it. It will pay off his debt. Like the man who set the wing alight. That time it was fourteen years. This time will be a week in the seg. If he doesn't fall off. Fall through more cracks and into my lap later. So officers stand around the perimeter and try to talk him down. As balance against the ongoing incident, everyone else has to be still. Still in class. Still safe. Until the incident is contained, we are.

You can taste the atmosphere again. What's happening? Where is it? Keep away from the windows. Stay in your seats.

One by one the other classes merge, bleeding into my space as colleagues rush out to ask for escorts. Smelling the chance to play games, Dean is once more in the room as the minutes slip into an hour. They've exhausted every trick I have. And I am more pit pony than show pony. We're onto games again now. Hangman is again a popular choice – you couldn't make it up. They could, though. The quietest learners spark into life with fantasy films and classic literature. Then it's on to guess the celebrity. The air is awash again with the faint smell of pasties. Dean moves around the room handing out coffees. Normally forbidden, but these were tricky times. His influence is also keeping things from bubbling over. Baubles of sweat prickle around the edges. Blurring the boundaries. Fear or excitement? Or both? Masks given by others slip from faces over weak, instant coffee. Charades offer veiled jokes to break the surface tension.

'Am I a man?'

'We have wondered, mate.'

'Am I on TV?'

'Only *Crimestoppers* and *Judge Judy*.'

'She's well fit, she is.'

'I've been on *Police Camera Action!* twice. Not that Jeremy Kyle tosser, though. Vile man. Exploits people and leaves 'em hangin'.'

'Am I Madeleine McCann?'

'We've found her! Do you reckon it was her parents? Is it because they are white? And rich? Summat ain't right there.'

And there it was. The patriarchy, judiciary, and class system succinctly summed up in four words as Dean dangles words and legs over the table. His eyes stop their Wimbledon to-and-fro between the ones to watch and the windows. Sweat has unstuck his Post-it note more than once as he slides between cracking jokes and worried looks.

We steer seamlessly between summative sociological analysis and *Sun* headlines for another thirty minutes until a cry of 'Oh my God, I wanted to be Katie Price!' almost drowns out the call to release for lunch.

'*Release from Labour and Education.*'

'Thanks, Miss. Safe.'

'Thanks, Kate. See ya tomorrow.'

Chairs under tables. Shredded papers thrown into the bin. Spilled out to grab the remains of the brown-ringer day, stealing a little bit of my sunshine as they leave.

When the teachers leave, in twos like unruly school children, it's darker. I always try to leave with Anna, the formidable personal development teacher. There's a rustling in the plants along the path. I know it's not human as it follows us out. Something walks beside us. A small, brave scrap of hope maybe. The need for change. The ground staff have cut down all the new growth. It's no barrier to stop missiles, either. A jam jar thudded onto my toes last week. I'm hoping it's a rook, taken to foraging in the plants. We start stamping as we walk. To keep the rats away. The rat stomp is now officially adopted as the regulatory exit regime. I can still see them running alongside, picking up wrappers washed up by the tide of human life inside the wing. More like beavers in size, they have driven away all the cats and foxes, damming up the gullies around buildings. They resist the small green boxes and gather in small groups in corners. But they don't cross our path. Not until much later.

'How was your week? Mine was murder. So much to do and not even time, as ever. Did I tell you that the beautician double-booked again? Nightmare. I mean, I'd go elsewhere, but she's just so cheap. And after the hot tub repairs, I just can't afford any more essentials this week. So that's where we are.'

Lynne sips her mochachocalattefrappalappadingdong, or whatever it's called. A merciful break in the torrent of words meaning everything and nothing.

'Anyway, I've been meaning to catch up and find out how things are. What's going on with the house? Must be a total nightmare having to travel and keep everything going. I do hope you are finding some time for yourself and not taking on too much. Oh, by the way, did you get around to that sewing I gave you last week? I could really do with that dress being taken in as I'm going to a do. Boring work thing obviously, but still. Have to keep up appearances.'

'Sorry. Not had a huge amount of time. Between work and everything.'

I'm clutching a mug of tea, which is becoming more acrid as it sinks. They've left the bag in as punishment for asking for something so dull. The smell coils down my throat, pulling at my heartstrings, reminding me of that empty home.

'Oh, that's fine. The do isn't until Saturday, so I'll pop over sometime tomorrow, yes?'

'That's fine.'

I shouldn't have offered. That'll teach me. Remembered habits learnt from a seamstress grandmother. The rhythm of the needle is somehow soothing. Even the sharp needle stab reminds me of the lessons she taught me. My dad's mum.

'And how are things with you? No, really. Tell me. It must be so difficult. You need someone to talk to properly and I'm here for you. Absolutely. I do need to get back for six o'clock though.'

'It's been OK.' It hasn't. 'Work keeps me out of trouble, you know?' It doesn't. 'It's the routine I need. Makes me get up each day, put clothes on. They can spot any weakness. Did I tell you I went in with my dress inside out last week? Proper embarrassing. Still, gave us all a laugh.'

'Why are you still even at that place? I can't understand it. It's no place for someone like you.'

Here we go again. 'How do you mean "someone like me"?'

'Well, you know. Nice. It's no place for a woman, either. All the violence. It must get to you. To see it and be reminded about how dangerous it is. How rough they are. It's all around you.'

'To be honest, Lynne, the only unseemly thing I have seen this week has been at Dad's house.'

Now half my house. I own the empty space appearing between the rotting food and books. A slice of the stale stuck, hovering above. Still. But try telling the grabbing, circling vultures. I prefer the prison rooks.

'Ooh, do tell. Have they been causing trouble again? Because you just have to say the word and I will be there. Your . . . what do you call it now? Wing-lady. For sure. Just not this next weekend – did I say we're going glamping again?'

'Trust me, I know people.'

We laugh. Covering up the reality of what could be. Who I know. What might be if I were the sort to be tempted.

'It's OK, thanks. I just don't think they realise. The box of books I'd taken from the shelves and laid by the door. I swear someone moved it. Rearranged it. Like I needed supervising. Checking I wasn't stealing. Daft thing was, most of them were mine anyway.' He had a habit of borrowing books to look at later. Never.

'Bloody cheek! They're yours to do with as you want! Can you not have a word?'

'I have several words. Most involve the letter "f". But it's not that simple. It never is.'

And that's not how it was, anyway. Boxes everywhere and no real order to it. Scattered memories and double-heart-handling everything. I'd left the box in the way and things had shifted. Lines in the sand redrawn. I was prickly tired and not seeing straight. Eyes used to watching were glazed over by the journey there. My ability to remember and re-member my self was already slipping away like a blood-soaked box bottom spilling its guts on the floor. And we hadn't even got to the hospital sickly-sunshine-yellow bags yet.

'Good riddance to them!'

'No. They're all that's left now.'

The ones that remain. The ones who can remember the gaps I can't. The stories I wasn't told. I've lost the plot and will cling to the final act's cast if it kills me. It just might. Holding on and letting go pull me apart. Faced with a hoarder's dream comfort blanket, the urge to scream becomes muffled in the noise of the clothes holding the musky earth smell, the old piano, the churning stalled car, the firearms, the chemicals, the five broken TVs, the piles and piles of mouse-dropping-filled papers. The crammed rooms layered with life and dust. Three houses held in one because they couldn't let go, either. The bright yellow plastic layer is the one I am most scared of. Carried back laundry in lieu of a wife having radiotherapy. Holding on to radioactive remains.

'Humph.'

Lynne's sermon is over. She's finished her fancy coffee and the next shop is calling her credit card's name.

'I don't think it's hit any of us yet, anyway.'

It's not real. It's not real. It's not happening. It hasn't happened. There were no police. No firemen. No blue lights. No reports. No doctors. No coroner. No funeral director.

'Well, it won't do, will it? Can't stand funerals myself. Won't get me near one. Not even family ones. Of course, I'll be there if you need me. When is it again? Hopefully not the end of the month. Did I tell you Sue wants to lend us her Airbnb? No? I must have. So nice to get away. Driving away from everything is so refreshing, isn't it?'

But in my head, I am already there. Bare walls and brown velvet curtains. He's back with us. I don't want them to draw the curtains yet.

When we arrive the next morning, the clouds are gathering. Loitering with intent. Nothing suspicious enough to make the cameras move. Just us, then. Time for a coffee and a gossip with my colleagues. The older, more battle-scarred staff were always in early and left on time. I am more battle-scared now. This time is a way of re-compressing. Of getting back into character. Approachable but wary. Shedding family moments and friends' names that might give someone a way in. Something to work with. The men shouldn't have phones, but they do. A week after I started, one asked if I liked Birmingham. For some reason, my Facebook page says I live there. I don't and never have. Like a bad teacher, I have never corrected it. Maybe it says somewhere more exotic now. I hope you don't see where. Where I'd like to be. Anywhere but here. My social media settings are on the highest privacy level. My friends' accounts clearly are not.

Inside, friendship is on different terms. Closer in times of danger, yet I can't (and wouldn't) tell you any of their personal details. We all look out for each other. Hearts lurch if a familiar voice calls for assistance. We share names of men who we have taught and what has worked for them. Don't wear red. Let them sit near the door. Use green paper for the class materials. Remove the food. Especially if it's Ramadan, to show respect.

Check the pens in and out. My new recruit has been thrown off the bricklaying course for demolishing the classroom. Built like a brick shithouse, he kicked over a display wall. Clearly all he needed was Northern charm and how to explain it in linguistic terms. An oxymoron. Some teachers share too much. I never like hearing the end of sentences.

'He's the one who—'

'For fuck's sake, John. You know I don't want to know.'

'Why? You need to know he is high risk.'

'Most of them are at risk of something.' Becoming violent. Homeless. Addicted. Reunited. Reconnected. Reborn. Returned. 'I still don't want to know.'

There are no detailed risk assessments. Clean slate and dirty floor. But it's still a nicer floor to look at that the one back home. His home. Now my home without him. Now invaded by others. Trampling over my past. Rifling through my memories held in boxes, books, and the smell of airlocked rooms.

'He's the one who—'

Don't finish that sentence. Stay here. In the place where time stands still. I quite like it here. No one can touch us. No touching. No feeling. Just connections. Don't tell me. There are things I would rather not know. Particular information is useful. Chef said there was a bad batch of Spice doing the rounds. He wasn't talking recipes. More Code Blues and Reds. Come to think of it, the night staff looked weary. Nothing much to report, aside from the usual staff assault, intimidation, and a kettling. We slurp another dark coffee. These were all in a day's rumblings. If these didn't happen, then something bigger was looming. Never jinx it by saying how quiet it is. You'd think quiet would be welcomed.

Writing this, I realise how I had normalised so much already. Because it meant survival. Getting through relied on being prepared. Turning suspicion into practical strategies was a different skill entirely. I hovered dangerously between vigilance and planned-for chaos.

'*Release for Labour and Education.*'

'Kate!'

'Did I forget my handouts again?'

'He's the one who got life for killing his female teacher.'

Up against the wall as they push in, all the scars and encounters with officials are held against me and my colleagues. All teachers are crap. Or worse, liars who pretend to care. All coppers, bent. All lawyers, on the make. All officers, Nazis. All the men here are innocent. How dare the judge not let them change from their work clothes to a suit. Who wouldn't jail a man in a black hoodie standing next to a bagged balaclava? Imagine finding him in your bedroom?

'Been different with a suit. Jury was led, Miss.'

'You lot are to blame.'

Look. Listen. Look again. I'm crossing over.

'What if it was your mother or wife?' I don't like using those words as it makes us relative to men. More valuable, perhaps. But it works inside.

'Don't bring them into it, Miss. I'm just a creeper. Burglary, like. They can afford it.'

My skin is creeping. Sliding down my back and trying to leave. Slip out quietly. I can feel it in my bones. This man is very, very broken. And I don't have any of the pieces. I'm not sure anyone has. For his Masters, he gave a video essay: 'Car Chases on *Police Camera Action!* ' He will soon receive a life-time fellowship for services to time management.

'Is that how you justify what you do? Really?'

'Only do it when I have to. One-man crime wave, me.'

Oh, to wave him goodbye. He has already held me personally responsible for Ardo's disappearance. It was a chance to yell about the system. I couldn't pretend he felt any empathy. Perhaps I sold him short. My second brain rises to my throat every time we share a room. My first brain sinks, knowing he will add another fail to my average results. And I have to get an 85% or above pass rate. In an average of twenty-seven hours interrupted teaching. Just how to write the basics. Read an advert and answer questions. Have a short discussion. They're brilliant at talking. If the topic is immigrants. Taking all the jobs, apparently. The jobs they won't do or can't do.

'So would you refuse medical treatment from a person who didn't have the same skin colour as you?'

'Knock me out first. Or shoot me.'

An image of his outline in white, coloured in with LGBTQI+ rainbows, flickers up. I push it back. Not very kind.

'Right. Or, should I say, wrong. Very wrong. Right, let's get on with the class. Yes, free speech means you can think what you want. But it does not entitle you to voice racist or homophobic views. If you do, I will shut you down.'

Lock you down. Why am I not allowed tape in class? Even if it doesn't seem to bloody work.

'Nah, Miss. You got me wrong. I love lesbians. This film I saw—'

'Christ on a bike!' My turn to swear. 'Will you pack it in? Get on with the work. Stop taking the piss. You are always on the take.'

'It's all there is on my CV.'

'Well, let's start again with your name and address.'

'*Education class break. I repeat, Education break.*'

Break off. Break out in a sweat as they pour out onto the landing outside the classroom. Dash to the loo. Grab a coffee. Steal a biscuit, unseen. Liz, the maths teacher, is already there. The staffroom is a calm oasis behind a locked door. Her class are in initial default scatter mode, too. Often their protection mechanism. But they have buried hearts and minds and will settle once they feel safe. They will thaw or leave. Masks and faces will be swapped either way. We talk about what we've noticed in their first hour. Dyslexia, dyscalculia, ADHD, SEMH, speech disability, visual and hearing loss, possible autism. There are twelve men total across our two classes. Now add in that their total hours in a school environment is about forty years. They were all lost at around eight years old. Stolen from the system. Fallen or pushed. I can see it would be easier to not have them in class. But now there is nowhere left for them to go. I can't and won't exclude them. They are the ones I like the most.

'*Resume Education. I repeat. Resume Education.*'

As Liz and I walk across the landing, my class seem to be in a rush to get back. Unusual. Warily refreshing even. Her door is open. Wide open. Shit. It's been ransacked. Speakers pulled off walls. Juice and stationery not just moved, but gone entirely. High cables hang like wispy lifelines from the walls. We have to call it. Report it. Officers arrive to assess it. No one saw anything. No one heard nothing. Sightlines conveniently forgotten.

The men are exchanging looks across the tables. The delightful creeper is particularly keen to get his head down to some work. He has a carrier bag under his chair. No one else looks happy. No one else speaks. Heads hang.

'What's in the bag?'

'Nothing, Miss.'

'Looks a very heavy nothing.'

He glares. I didn't think his beady little eyes could get narrower.

'Just an Xbox my friend borrowed.'

'What friend?'

'Don't you mean "Which friend?"'

Ah, so now you want to do grammar. Hide behind distractions. Look over there, Miss, it's a good student. The others shift in their seats.

'Does anyone have anything to say?'

Of course they don't. And I don't really expect them to.

The officers are still in the building. I swallow back bile. Acrid. Burning. This isn't going to be easy. Prickling fingers meet sticky fingers. Snitches get stitches.

'You know you will all get your cells spun, don't you?'

Five out of six faces fall out of line for a second. I hesitate to think why. What else will be found? Maybe it's a good thing. I imagine my face blistering. That sweet sliding skin smell.

'So. To stop that happening, I am going to ask the officer if he will search each of you on the way out. Is that OK?'

'Whatever stops you moaning, Miss.'

As they line up, I notice that the carrier bag has disappeared. Magic. Each man has to stand, arms outstretched, Christ-like, whilst they are patted down. Good men. Well done. Then they leave, puffing back up as they go through the door. It was difficult to watch. A reminder of where we are and what has to be done to protect the innocent. They didn't look angry. Shrinking or mocking. Offering to show us all their junk. Nowhere to hide. I didn't look away quick enough. Not the first time I had seen a flaccid penis proudly dangled in the education block. Nothing to see there. Nothing to find.

We searched the unit for any of the missing items. Behind posters. Under displays. On the top of storage units. We even braved the toilets. Not a smell Dior will be copying anytime soon. We found doubts over whether the door had been locked.

It had. Over what we were doing. We were doing OK in arguably the most challenging place to teach. We found reminders to not treat anyone as an equal. To lose trust. To lose part of what it is to be human. Until the next morning. Dean bounded in with the bag full of speakers and other items. Found on the step, he said. Only cables that would be charging illicit phones were missing. No questions asked or answers given. There was some honour amongst thieves after all.

By the end of a strained six-week course, I had learnt to lock up all my resources at the end of each day. A smaller prison for the words of hope and future employment. But I had survived without the shit hitting the fan, walls and face, the customary punishment for staff who had offended: *'Please do not call the office phone in block D as it is currently covered in excrement.'* Besides, the fan was long gone after a warm weekend. There were some students I was happy to lose. To release back into the wild. And off he went. Yelling about the EDL. Which isn't an electricity company. Trying to ignite a response. I told him I didn't want to see him again. It's actually what I tell them all.

5.

Lesson 6 of 20: Duration 2hrs.

Learners: 8.

Levels: Functional Skills E1–L2.

Additional Notes: ADHD, SEMD, PTSD. Some in combination. No break. Hold on to your head, heart, pens, and pee.

Aims and Outcomes: Nobody dies. Not today.

It seems quite flippant. A basic premise for any human interaction. To preserve life. That we all walk out of the space alive. Maybe a few egos bruised but otherwise intact. In a secure unit, the expectation might be lower. Actual cuts and bruises. Worst case: broken bones. That was just the team-building meetings.

John is on holiday so no jokes and banter to part the morning gloom. I throw a couple of Nurofen down my throat as the car stops. Engine stalled. This space will do. I nod to the officers putting their belts on in the car park and walk across the path.

'Mobile disco has arrived.'

'Just because it's better than your Barry Manilow, eh, Smithy.'

'Ouch. I'm hurt. How could you?'

'I think that every day, mate.'

'See you on the inside, Miss.'

'Miss you already.'

Still no first name. Not quite been inside long enough to warrant the effort perhaps. Teachers left after days or never even arrived. Most were gone after six months. What am I doing here? Time to forget the privilege of a university life and the washed-up house of memories far away. Leave it all behind like the emergency £20 note stashed under the car seat. Leave it and the world behind. Work with what remains when everything else is taken away. Leaving my phone in the car has always felt risky, even after the shaking stopped. But having broken down in more ways than one on the way home last week, it was comforting to have it there. Help was a call away. Clutch at straws. Some weeks are better than others. Or is it that all weeks are the same; I just cope better some days?

Today I have a skeletal lesson plan. Skin and bones of how to get through. To be fleshed out by how the men adapt to the material. Student-centred learning. Responsive. Plus I have given up detailing ideas in minutiae. Things can change in an instant. A phone call. A stray word. A loose idea scampering across the tables. Stray learners. An event outside the walls. A letter bringing news in. Turns a lesson inside out. Gut-lurching moments and heartfelt triumphs. When someone passes their first ever exam. At the age of fifty-six. When a man becomes a peer mentor to others. When you hear a man sounding words out and learning to read his children's names. Every literacy method is greeted by:

'Tried that one, Miss.'

'Hated that one.'

'I'm not a bleedin' child, you know.'

'Nah. Not again.'

'What's the point – am sixty-seven, Miss. No point.'

'Stop wasting your time with me.'

'Can't get it into me thick head. After hospital, my head don't work. No use rememberin.'

Wait. My numb brain flickers to life. 'What do you mean, hospital?'

'Coma. Someone done me head with a hammer.'

'Jesus. How long did it take you to recover?'

'Stitches and all, about a year I lost.'

'That would explain why you can't remember things. Let's work with what you can see and hear and say.'

'I'm grand at talking. Me kids love a good story.'

'How many do you have?'

'Turteen.'

'Lucky for us.'

'Do you know what their names look like?'

'Just about. Me wives chose most of dem.'

'Let me write them down. You can keep the paper safe in the cabinet. No one will see them.'

His prickly stubble softens. 'All right, Miss. As it's for you, right enough.'

I wrote down their names in order and he agreed each one's spelling by sight. Between them, they contained all the phonetic sounds we needed. After that he could sound words out. Put them together. Remember their shapes and sounds. Remember how far we'd got. His children taught him to read.

Remembering nicer moments pushed me back inside. It was easier to ignore the piles of books my dad had left me, scribbled margin notes and well-creased words told over torchlit bedtimes. They were miles away. I'd been ghosted from the house and all it held. A hoard of stories tied in string and baby teeth. He had kept everything and I wanted none of it. The food tins piled high like a lifer's cell. The yellow pictures out of time and mind. The twice-breathed air lingering around the door frames. The doors with bolts on the outside. Where the fear of losing leaves no room for holding onto people. Capturing moments in objects coveted. Words unspoken as the hoard buried us. I can't see him for the exploded tins of fruit kept just in case. Hungry for attention while pushing back prying eyes. Hidden hungers.

Prison is an uncanny refuge. I've packed a small lunch. Approaching the gate, I'm glad I wasn't organised this morning. Normally, I would bring in a multipack of cereal, and lunch pots. Whatever could be eaten whilst in a meeting or over a rare chance to use the computer. Just one between seventeen of us, within limited internet access and the slowest wheel of doom scrolling round the screen. Bringing in large quantities of food is seen as suspicious. You'd be surprised how many phones will fit in a box of cornflakes. Six in the set to collect. The one as small as a Mars bar. The large screen iPhone – ideal for arranging a deal. On special offer – ten years extra free. Staff stories whisper through the trees as we line up.

Today is already different. No being sucked into the airlock and spat out of the other side today. Today we are waiting to go in, escorted in twos. Guided through the visits entrance. Do not pass Go. Do not collect keys and a radio. Wait to be called in. Stand in a line, a metre apart. The dogs will be walked in between you and the person in front. Sit down. Do not pet the dog or distract the dog. He is working. He sniffs the contents of my bag. Just one Pot Noodle. Well-sealed. Like my mouth. Don't make jokes. Next stop the larger room. Put your bag on the table. An officer empties the contents and goes through everything. Scrutinises every single piece of paper, receipt, and item. A line of metal thermos cups is growing along the front desk. Confiscated. Someone is taken aside. They have more than £60 in old £20 notes. Asked questions. Sniffed by dogs. Something smelt off.

'Over here, miss. Put your hands by your sides. Don't move. Look straight ahead. Now go through to the next room.'

'Stand here. Take off your coat and shoes. Odd socks. Remove your belt. Arms up. Feet apart.'

Pockets gone through. Linings checked. Slowest pickpocket ever. Now I am about to know exactly how every visitor feels. Every child, wife, brother, father, and mother that comes through the doors, following the path of the little monsters painted on the floor.

'Stand with your legs apart. Arms out straight. Don't move.'

Don't laugh or try to crack a joke. Stern faces and firm, blue-gloved hands. Patted up one leg and then down the other. Then body and arms.

My utility belt is emptied onto the chair.

'I hope you're going to put all that back. It's like Tetris.'

Glares.

Flicks through my purse, holding an old receipt up to the light, smelling the single £5 note.

'Good luck finding any cash in there.'

Weak I've-heard-that-too-many-times-today smile.

Attention turns to my inhaler. Pulled apart. Narrowed eyes.

'It's been cleared.'

No smiles given or taken.

'That's fine. Please leave by that door.'

Scoop up your things, clutch them to your chest, and scurry out like a guilty lover caught in the act. Straighten yourself out, smooth over the creases, crumpled feelings pushed into the corners of your bag. Belt back on. But the normal is now in reverse. Walk back to the start. But time has gone forward. I've lost thirty minutes already. Collect the keys from your favourite box. Then the radio. Check the battery. And out into the estate.

With just a glimpse of what they have been through to get here. Guilty until proven innocent.

Nothing to hide here. No white powders slipped into books. No sprayed paper or tablets in the coffee. Nothing plugged. Words stuffed into the cracks of my limbs as they shake off the last half an hour. Time lost. Trust gained, perhaps. People can change, though. Some for the better. Others, not so much. Onto the day in hand. Fingers clutch a coffee mug.

'Biscuit? Wasn't chocolate until I plugged it.'

'No thanks very much.'

'Thought not. More for me.'

'Anyone need the photocopier?'

'Is the computer free?'

'Release for Labour and Education.'

Another lesson is being notched up on the wall. A football moves across a green pitch chart on its way to the goal. We've done OK today. Ambled through grammar, a formal letter, and language features. Logos are always useful for learning the rule of three. Each man is given a logo. Then they have to give the tagline. It is always three words.

'Every little helps.'

'Miss. Is it time to leave yet?'

'Just do it.'

'For the many.'

'Miss. I'm lovin' it.'

'I could murder a burger right now.'

'Aren't you veggie, Miss?'

'Why?'

'Couldn't live without bacon.'

'Finger lickin' good.'

'Not the few.'

'Unless it's Ramadan.'

'Miss. What's that banging?'

'Probably the pipes. You know the toilets are next door.'

'Can I go?'

'It's only a few minutes until the end. Can't you tie a knot in it? It's not long.'

'You been staring again, Miss?'

'Cease Labour and Education.'

Pack it up. Chairs under. Pens in. Let's go.

'Code Blue Education.'

As they go down the stairs, I feel the rumble of boots under my feet. There are more footsteps rushing towards us. I usher my learners out. Try to discreetly move the grey tide aside to let the black and whites through. I return to my classroom. The officers are gathering on the landing. A colleague comes out of her class with one of her learners. He is swaying. Staring. Wide-eyed and unable to walk properly. The officers let them sit down on the scruffy chairs. He sinks into the blue, then rises with hands holding his arms and face. His eyes roll white into the back of his head and shudder back. The room is spinning with Liam at the epicentre. Tables, desks, books, and trolleys settle to the floor. The officers pull away and let Anna as his teacher sit beside him. Mumbling forms into words. He begins to talk. Of his fears and of the hardships on the wing. He is being bullied into persuading his brother to bring in drugs. Their next family visit is being hijacked.

Gestured to stay back, I watched from my doorway. It is the first time I have seen the aftermath of a Spice attack. As his head stops spinning, mine starts. He is still tottering as he goes back to the wing. But he is breathing. Moving. Still alive.

This is the first time I haven't seen Dean after class. He's slipped away into the night. Something isn't right. I mean in the grand scheme of things. Nothing is right in prison. Shades of grey, blurred lines, and red puncture wounds.

Over the course of the next four months, there were as many deaths. Three were attributed to the drug Spice. Readily available in prison. As a legal high it was £1 a packet. Then it was outlawed. Inside, it cost much more. It cost bruises, money, and lives. Men told stories of what happened whilst under its influence. Climbing walls, walking zombie-like, heads smashing open after falling. Heads smashed in after failing to pay up. Collections due the day of canteen. No recollection of what happened. Of one who cut off his own penis and found it floating in the toilet after he woke up on the floor. What a dickhead. It had always happened to someone's brother's friend's padmate. Tales aside, what we knew was that there was a high risk of sudden death. They could drop to the floor and stop breathing in seconds. A football game had turned into a game of sleeping lions for one team when three players fell to the ground outside my classroom. Medical support was standard procedure as soon as you suspected a man was under the influence. Nurses would be seen rushing across the estate with the oxygen on their backs, wheezing into residential wings to get to another collapse. The system was being brought to its knees.

Men would take it to escape the realities of their daily lives inside. For a bet. To settle a debt. Be spiked for others' entertainment. It was more potent thanks to the smoking ban. No longer sprinkled with tobacco, it was smoked in altered vapes, tea bags, or even with grass cuttings. Plants were stripped of leaves when a new batch of Spice arrived. Heady smells of leaves and pure Spice lurked around cells. Secondary inhalation was also a risk to staff. Different 'brands' were distinctive. Fragrant, perfumed coils seeped into beds and blankets. Monkey Dust was well-known as a quality product from my hometown, unlike the versions that were manufactured in prison. Spice came in on paper. Sprayed on children's pictures, letters, doubling the value of old £20 notes. It came over the fence and under the radar. In children's toys, on visits, by drone, and in person. Literally.

Other drugs roamed the wings. Heroin and ketamine among other suspects. As were the prescription meds that were cheeked for later. Games of pass the parcel through the burnt-out shell of C Wing. Yells of delight as a layer of paper from a water-soaked cell revealed a prize, before the officers and dog gave chase. No chance of ball games. The object of that game was to pass drugs inside the ball between players. The goalposts were always moving when it came to the drugs game. When one chain was closed down, another opened up. Through closed windows and locked doors. Hollowed-out library books, empty eyes, and goosebump skin all found their way into my class. I learnt to notice the side-wobbling head, sweat-beaded skin. And raised, bumpy chicken skin that meant a man was in withdrawal. Clucking. But chickens made the best students.

As a teacher, you are not supposed to have a favourite student. But here I am going to tell you the truth. Not quite the whole truth, but nothing but the truth. I had several students who made me really smile. Paul used to arrive every morning, bobbing into class with ruffled feathers. He had always got out of the wrong side of the bed. Which was impressive given that his was fixed to the wall.

'I've had a crap morning. Can I leave?'

'Paul, you've only just arrived. Have a seat. Here's a quick puzzle.'

'It's me head. Not slept.'

'Neither have I, if I'm honest.'

'Actually, you're alright you are. What do I do next?'

'Give out the paperwork and pens?'

'Need to keep going. Proper cluckin' today.'

'As in KFC?' I search for what he means.

'Look. Me skin, like.'

'More goose than chicken.'

'Alright, smart-arse. What can I do next?'

'We're missing a few.'

'Not the only thing we're missing.'

'I don't suppose you fancy writing a short story?'

'Nope.' He's on his feet already. A little wobbly but in earnest. 'How short would it have to be? We're talking words, Kate.'

'How about six?'

'I'd need more than that, mind.'

'No. You can have six.'

'I've had a rough morning, Kate. You ain't helping.'

'Here's an example: nothing like this had happened before.' Not the Hemingway 'For sale. Baby shoes. Never worn.' None of us can face that story. Stillborn stories of miscarriage find their voice elsewhere, in gardens and yards, even in a men's prison.

'Are you having a laugh?'

'That's only five words.' I grin. The others are arriving after being caught behind their doors following an incident.

'Are you taking the piss?'

'Still stuck on five, then.'

'Teachers do my head in.'

'Still five. Add an adjective.'

'Nothing changes.'

'Nope. It just stays the same.'

'Now you're on five, Kate.'

'If nothing changes . . . then nothing changes. Boom!'

'Right. Next thing. Let's do this.'

Paul slips between articles, reports, and spelling challenges like an electric eel. He keeps me on my toes. Scratching around for little pieces of gold to keep him focused. Every morning has to be different. A haiku, cinquain, acrostic. Always greeted by a 'What the fuck's that?' Always followed by writing.

By the end of the course, we had written twenty pieces together. He taught me the value of the creative moments. The stories we told ourselves. The ones we hid in metaphors or held up to let the light shine through. When he left, his eyes were as clear as glass. And so were mine. It was obvious that, for better or for worse, I wanted to be with the ones who were the most difficult to reach. The ones bound in layers of stories. In smoke and mirrors.

The decision to leave the relative safety of the classroom wasn't a particularly wise one, but I needed to not be in that room. The space where my world fell apart. I needed a gap year. Time out. But I couldn't afford it. So I went for a work placement option. One working for the prison on the wings. I offered to work with the men that didn't get to leave the wings. I knew there were men who would never be able to find their way to the education building. The self-isolators didn't leave their cells. Some refused the half-hour time slot to be let out for a shower and grab a tray lunch. Debt, fear, anxiety, illness all kept them from seeing the light of day. And being stubbornly unphased by a challenge, I started on the segregation wing.

Where everything had been taken away. Bare walls. Few possessions. Nothing to hide behind.

It has taken a few attempts to get the timing right. I step aside to let in six officers carrying a furious man to a cell. The sight of officers in white biohazard suits accompanying a man covered in his own faeces delays my visit again. Shit. What have I done? When I do get through the gate, the officers seem surprised anyone would want to be here. No one had bothered before. We talk through how it could work. The staff office is within sightlines of two small rooms. If the judge wasn't using them to adjudicate on extra time for crimes committed inside the prison, I could use that table. Only with the door open. This is not a place for pushing boundaries. This is the last place you want to become a liability. They already call me Snowflake.

When the yelling starts, I stop. Stand still. Feel useless. Step back. The governor is summoned. When he arrives, he has brought his family dog with him. He hands Bentley to me and goes to the cell door. And here we are, Bentley and me. Either end of a lead. Wide and tired-eyed. A portly chocolate Labrador and a scrawny Northerner exchanging unknowing glances and sighs. As the cell door opens, a sink flies out and hits the wall opposite. Metal bounces surprisingly well. Mangled pipes weep in pain. The door is rapidly shut until four officers return with shields. Stepping over the pool of water leaking out from under the door, they go back in. Calming words from the governor and all is quieter. The door is still open. So I ask if he is OK to talk to. Officers shrug. Why not? So I go in. Introduce myself and ask if he wants anything. To distract him. Keep him occupied. As maintenance arrive to put the sink plumbing back in, we talk. Make eye contact. Even smile. I leave him with one book and a chapter of another. There are questions to think about. Not the big ones about history, origins, and how we have got to this place. Just ones based on the words he holds in his hand. Words we can start with next week until we find our own. A long-distance reading group. No pen allowed. I've already taken the staples out of the papers.

The cell opposite is opened for me to loiter by the door and ask if the man inside is OK. He smiled.

'Another day in paradise, Miss.'

'Would you like something to do? An activity pack maybe? Some writing?'

'Actually . . .'

'What?'

'You won't laugh?'

'Can't promise.'

'I want a book.'

'Not laughing yet.'

'Shakespeare.'

'Now that I didn't expect. Sorry. Says a lot about me and how little I have learnt so far. Which one?'

'I don't know. The one with a hero.'

'Have you seen it before?'

'No, Miss. I only saw bits. Want to know how to write one.'

'That I can help with.'

'Say what? Really? Fuck me.'

'No thanks. We'll leave the shagging for Shakespeare.'

Once a week, he was let out of his cell for an afternoon of Shakespearean tragedy. Unlocked. Both of us. We spoke of action, flaws, and family history. Moments of realisation. Of the inevitable fall from grace. Hamlet, Othello, and Macbeth. We skipped how to manipulate an audience, focusing on safer ideas of intention and how it can be misread. He taught me about flow and rhythm. I showed him how to find his voice. It came from close family ties and breaking free from expectations. Becoming a painter and decorator. Or a playwright. His monologue had all the right ingredients. The man as a political citizen, the rise and fall of hope. His mental health improved. He stopped the dirty protests. Much to the officers' pretend annoyance that they had lost their extra shitting-up allowance. Writing on walls was exchanged for a small exercise book and pen. We joked that I wrote shit poetry. We didn't get to the ending. He was shipped out. Ghosted. Back to the beginning. A spirit on the ramparts. To be or not to be inside. That was the question.

The neighbour he never met was my next student. He had been recommended to me. He needed something creative. He enjoyed writing. As we talked through the bars of the exercise yard, he spoke of words, reading, and the need for something. Anything to take him away. Anywhere but all the places like here he had been before. His eyes were glazed. Skin clammy to the eye. It wasn't that warm in the small quadrangle. Here was my next project. Turns out he thought the same thing.

Even on the segregation unit, walls within walls, Jimmy had managed to get drugs. As he fought his way off them, we wrote of times past, present, and future. He was moved to F Wing. The one with a garden and chickens. This once violent addict would cradle a chicken under his arm as he wrote. He had names for them all and he unlocked their run each time he saw they had been caged. He stole strawberries from the small garden plot to hand feed his girls. These chickens joined us on a picnic bench in the sun, doubling the numbers. Our tattoo armour signalled not to go too deep. Inked skin spoke of past traumas. Their silent stories sat unspoken. We began with the objects of childhood: roller skates, broken biscuits, and flares. No distress signals there. Onto the present: gift books, art, and over-cooked food. The future was fantastic. Flying cars and freedom. With a chicken on each side, words shaped the world as we wanted it to be. Where chickens and rats scurried free. Where you didn't think about just how many phones and bags of drugs you could fit inside a dead one. Where bars were for beer and spice was for cooking. A world impossible.

6.

Lunchtime is the biggest misnomer in teaching. Not just prison teaching. There is neither time nor space for lunch. Lunchtime is for meetings. We are kept inside against our will at least twice a week. To enhance quality and build a team ethic. Quickly stuff sandwiches down our throats and scurry into the main room at the top of the stairs. And today there are the dreaded pens and large flipchart paper on tables. Passing notes, sniggering, refusing to step up, volunteering others. We make the worst students.

Amongst the sentences on strips of paper are indicators of excellence. Requires improvement. Adequate. Outstanding. My paperwork is always outstanding. Always late. I don't think that's what they meant. In the flurry of matching the words to the values, the paper strips tangle into a hamster bedding ball on the floor. Shredded performance dreams. Bending down to pick a familiar statement, my foot slips and my hand darts out to steady my descent into the maelstrom of quality measures. Flicker of sharpness. Nervous laugh and back up again. Totally meant to do that.

By the time I turn into the drive at home, my hand is cradled in my lap. Sleepless newborn cries can only mean a hospital trip. Falling asleep in the drool pool on the sofa will have to wait.

'It doesn't look broken but let's X-ray it anyway.'

More waiting. Dinnertime becomes the next sequel in the misnomer series. As does suppertime.

'Ah, there we are. That crack there. It's a stress fracture of the hand. You've broken your fingers before, too.'

That would have been an altercation with a red phone box door.

'Do I need a cast? Can I still go to work?'

'We can put you in a brace, but it has to stay on for six weeks. Minimum.'

'That's only the length of one course. That's OK, I guess.'

Hand brace Velcro screeches into place and we are back home to darkness. Husband has sulked all the way there and back. He knows it will take more than broken bones to stop me going in.

Six hours later, buoyed by painkillers, and eight men scatter into the room.

'Miss, you look like shit.'

'Worse than my nan.'

'We really need to teach you how to pay a compliment.'

'I knows already. I could have said my paps.'

'What you done to your hand?'

'What does the other guy look like?'

'Last man to fail the exam, Miss?'

To disclose a weakness or not. A calculated risk, embedding maths in the lesson plan.

'Totally. He was a hard nut to crack.'

'Not a roadman then, Miss?'

Sniggers and laughter bubble up.

'Broken, is it?'

'Is it?'

'Let me hold the books for you.'

'Give out the sheets, my man there. Pass the pens.'

'Better count 'em back in again.'

'You've gotta watch out for thieves round here.'

'What's this, Miss?'

'An article on robot cars. Would you trust one? What about a robot teacher?'

'Nah. Bare breakdowns. Sorry, Miss. Didn't mean it, like.'

'Maybe we should focus on automated cars. Could there be advantages?'

'So man could deliver tings with the satnav?'

'In theory, yes. They have robots delivering shopping already.'

'And if the feds stopped it, man wouldn't be near ting?'

'That's what man's talkin' 'bout!'

'I see where this is going.'

Down the one-way road, the one well travelled.

'So do we, Miss. Man bare driving like Deliveroo on road.'

Sigh. 'Sadly, it's time for a break.'

Laughter. Spilling out of the door onto the landing. Upright man slumps and hangs low. Murmurs and outbursts whilst an orderly brings in blank certificates.

'Would you like to stay and explain to the men why these certificates have been brought in? To show positive behaviour in a place where it is easier to record the negative.'

'Absolutely. So there are certificates for attendance, participation, supportive behaviour, and progression. You can show them to your OMU, for probation and DCat reviews.'

'Swear down?'

'Really.' Buoyed by the wide-eyed looks, missing the tenuous hold on their gaze. 'I can do any certificates you want. Like The Best N***o on the Wing?'

Chairs scrape onto walls. Bolt upright and moving quickly from all sides.

'Get out! Now!'

Hold on. Hold back. It's not worth it.

Wide eyes darken with fury. Head pushing beyond the outstretched chest filled with fire and unleashed power. Broken hand on heart. My broken hand. His pain.

'Is it worth it? You'll be the one who gets a nicking. Think about it.' Do not push the button.

Either way, trouble lies. War on the wings or class battles. Slow release of hand from his beating, passionate heart.

'Miss. Get out of the way. He doesn't get to say that word. You don't understand.'

Push it back. Right back with broken bones and hurt pride. Simmer down. Stop for just a minute and think.

'Miss, he needs to come back. He needs to apologise. Or every man here will see him hurt.'

Murmured apology re-ignites.

'Sorry. It's just my culture.'

And we're off again. Tables are pulled apart and everyone seems taller. Wider and wide-eyed.

'Run! Get behind the door! Go!'

Caught between a man and passion, words don't fail me.

'Let's do this properly. The right way. If you batter him, then you will be charged. Recharge. Sit down. Please.'

Tables are moved back into line. Chairs pulled in by their legs and we talk.

'What do you want to happen?'

'Deal with it, Miss. Or we will.'

'Do you trust me?'

'For now.'

'I will report it. Fill in a DIRF – a racist incident.' Process the power of words into a small box. Paper aeroplanes across a great divide.

'Miss, we ain't in the mood.'

'I can understand that.'

After the class I talk through what's happened with Anna. My go-to mentor, wing-lady, and guru for all things official and under the radar.

So, that afternoon, we scurry next door to Anna's class. She teaches personal development courses on reducing violence. She already knows about the incident and she welcomes us in. She has a plan. To calm the pulsing veins and my throbbing hand. We're all just a bit more broken today. To give an outlet before they return to their wings. No stewing on the day's events over food. No punching walls or anyone unlucky enough to get in the way.

Next door to the scene of the crime we watch a video. Normally the recourse of a weary-worn teacher counting down the days to Christmas. Here, it's holding us together. A rare moment when a teacher has been allowed to bring in a film, screened twice by security and the college. Even in an adult prison, we are not allowed to use games or videos with an 18 certificate. This is a documentary about gang violence, Bloods and Crips across the pond but coming back in waves. It starts with sensational images and the audience puffs up in the mirror. Stop the scene. Here. Focus on the mothers' faces. The tears blur the edges. The Bloods' founding members speak of present history, future hauntings, and past events. Freeze frame. His eyes. Wider and emptier. How did they lose their fire? Blank but instantly readable. As he speaks, inscribed power lines flicker and connect to the group. Battle scars of class wars unseen to the privileged. Shots fired. Destination unknown.

The former soldier with PTSD sits silently in the middle of the group. White Northern and London Black African share the void and begin to fill the space. Trickled speech pools outwards.

'So what can we do now? How do we understand what is happening?'

'It's not about understanding, Miss. It's *over*standing the issues. My issues you made. Like Black History Month. Totally ignored. And it's only a month for you. But it's our whole life, Miss. Years and years of months, if we make it.'

And yet we are all together on this. Just for a moment, it's about class. This class. The lack of choices. The lack of visibility. Subjugation and culture intertwined.

'You have to understand where we come from. Where we have come from is not just about place. Where we don't belong. Where we were taken from. Where we are now. Look at this class. How many of us are Black? And bare poor. Foodbanks and pride don't mix, Miss.'

By October, there is a huge, shameful display of the history of slavery in the library. Men who are paid £11 a week to pack nuts and bolts into bags look on. Discomfort. Moving from one foot to the other. Bitten lips and nails.

'Why isn't there a White History Month, then?'

'Because you get every month, my dear.'

Every single day. Except for International Women's Day. And Herstory month. And other pronouns. I'm still looking. Would you pour water on every yard in the street when only one was on fire? Why is it that someone always comes off worse? Even in here, where there is a chance to start again. All begin equal, dressed the same and on the same footing within the perimeter fence. Prison strips away the veneer and exposes what makes a human weak or powerful. Names mean something. Be Lord of the Spiders or a nobody caught mid-flight. Existing unseen, voices invisible. Barely living with a new set of rules. Get potted. Two-for-one caps. Say nothing. Swear down. Catch you later, the fly heard. Unspoken rules. Here the invisible becomes visible in what remains of life. Illustrated men wearing trauma on their sleeves. Hierarchies of grey tracksuit brands where the gorilla logo is king. 'King you later', he says, before bang-up. When time moves in circles and walls close in. Where men try to deliberately work against the norm, free-flow walks anti-clockwise around the inner quadrant. The inner circles that mirror the corridors of power, where Kings, a few Queens, and the Jokers assert their positions in the pack. Ghosts of the living, they haunt the wings and float through walls. I wasn't there. No one saw me. Nobody sees me. Only I see you. In myself sometimes.

We try to build resilience. To manage the fine line between coping and resistance. I slowly increase the time they spend on tasks. Give them more responsibility for their own learning and then each other's. Group discussions are negotiated with care. Setting up debates actively pits them against each other. Pride is at stake. We navigate group contracts and behaviour awards. They set their own targets and are far harder on themselves than I would be. By the third week, they are ruthless at blind marking practice exams I have created. Tables are turning in minds rather than reality. We look at the difference between facts and opinions. Learn when a leaflet is biased or trying to sell something. Making false claims. Is it informative or persuasive? Blurred lines from court cases play out in the breaks. Performed for an audience before they get back into character for the lesson. Or do I see the face rather than the mask? I take it all at face value. But with the secret knowledge that this is one story of many. Heroes and villains are interchangeable, depending on which side of the gate you live. There is no sitting on the fence. Even if the estate is teeming with mobile grey areas. Men moving between home and work in a world within a world. Hidden from view. Your worst fears kept out of sight. Out of their minds.

'Wow. You look aaaawful. I already ordered.'

Two dark red paper cups soak up the silence for a second.

'Thanks. I needed that. What was it?'

'Double espresso. I knew I'd convert you sooner or later. How's things?'

'I am running on empty. Weekends at the house.' I still cannot say his name. 'It's just fucking endless.'

'I meant the hand. Who did that to you? Was it someone at work? You could sue. I know a fab lawyer friend who'd do it. Doesn't do mates rates but he's good.'

'Actually, I fell.'

'Mmmhmm. After walking into a door? Or was it a fist?'

'Nope. Definitely a floor. I even have a matching carpet burn to prove it, your honour. I got called a special someone for that.'

Only Lynne doesn't smile. She's somewhere else. That place I go to when the words pull me apart like horses dragging coal carts up to the light. That slow, pull stretch to find air.

And then we're both back in the coffee shop. Caffeine fumes and cash tills register the real world of now.

'Come on. I need to find a dress without any fucking buttons. No belt needed and preferably elastic.'

'You say the best things. I'll find a matching necklace.'

Of course, she hasn't remembered I can't wear any jewellery. I choke on the words and let it go, slipping back to them like an addict. The vacant pale eyes of the shop assistants remind me of Adam, who's been with me since the very beginning.

Adam had already served eight years longer than the standard tariff for his crime. He was disappearing before me, fading into a grey husk of a human being. Pale liquid blue eyes spoke of being moved from prison to prison. Wide-eyed witnessings and words failing him.

His story was written in blood and burns. Dots and dashes on his arms punctuated his progress as he struggled to feel anything but numb. He had overdosed on empathy and shut down. A closed colouring book of red and clotted black. This book you could judge by his cover. Wearing a sweatshirt while the classroom slowly parboiled its contents into a grumpy stew meant the bindings underneath were back. Prison-made bandages of socks and blue roll twisted into tight rings would need stitches later. Sticking plasters for a child come undone. A prison orphan. Like me, he had lost his dad whilst in prison.

For a different ending, he needed to show progress. Rewrite the patterns of lines waving goodbye to the gate. The relative quiet of the education block seemed to soothe him. So, Liz put together a plan for his recovery. He would be able to take our courses and then stay on as a peer mentor. He could flit between our classes, keeping busy in functional skills. Keeping him functioning without drugs and with an impending diagnosis. Slowly, his eyes raised and cleared, colour flickering into his veins when he pulled up a tatty chair next to another man. Sounding out words for the man next to him, his voice returned to strengthen mine. It still does.

We worked to hold him together while he healed. That made it difficult to pick at the edges. Sealing the deal with a diagnosis of autism that came thirty-five years too late to save his childhood. Thumbing through the lost chapters, self-editing distress signals, Adam began to inscribe stories on paper. He brought me the blue exercise book we had used for level two. In the margins, another story was emerging from the sentences. We agreed he should keep it in code for safety. The things he had inadvertently seen and suspicious prison eyes made it necessary. Another mask. But it worked to distance him from immediacy. Sharp stinging presence bled blue onto the page. His royal blood was a sign of standing amongst some. Possibly a lifer, he had a cell to himself. He was enhanced within a few months, filling in his outline with a little more gristle on the bone-tired frame.

The autobiography held him together. Sketched-out storied selves danced before us. Swirling smoke tutus wound around bodies. Skipped over blackouts and died before the curtain fell. Our story ended. No encore, as I never saw him again after he left. He had refused the calls to come back to the familiar, going solo for the outside sequel. Into approved premises which Liz had doggedly fought for. With a fighting chance, unlike the one released NFA. Three little letters that meant No Fixed Abode. The motto of a boomerang tribe, which I threw away to return travel wearied, caught in a home run circle.

Imagine being in self-isolation for ten years. In the middle of nowhere. Then emerging to a new world of phones, internet, social media. Even money has changed. The rules of engagement are unrecognisable. You can order food without leaving the house. You can swipe left or right to reject or find a date. Your location is traceable through your phone or CCTV. A quick Google search will reveal all your secrets. And a few lies as well. The world you knew has changed beyond recognition. So has your family. During your time inside, both your parents have died. Your partner has found someone else. Your children have been adopted by another man. You are now a stranger. In a strange land. With £50 and a flimsy bag with a few toiletries and an ill-fitting suit. No surprise that the prison seems a safer bet. Somewhere between the devil and the deep grey sea.

Desperation or debt drove some men to extreme lengths. I'd

met men who had deliberately self-harmed, assaulted staff, or kettled a cellmate in order to be moved to another prison. I'd seen the effect of these acts on reviews and records. It was all there in black and white. Safely on a screen. Histories at finger's length. Just out of reach. Until the day it came to our door. And ran rampage inside.

The simmering tensions of the estate sparked me out of the numbness grief waves washed over. You couldn't be complacent. The material for lessons was refreshed for each course. Whatever they expected, after gossiping with others on the wing, never quite tallied up. It kept them alert, too. Within the standard curriculum of letters, reports, articles, and grammar, the themes were tailored to their interests or away from their triggers. Articles on driverless cars were removed from men found guilty of causing death by dangerous driving. Housing reports vanished for those who were inside just to avoid homelessness. Food recipes were swapped for business proposals during Ramadan. Alarms went off in the buildings next to us. On other wings. Locking my classroom door at the end of the day brought a sigh of relief alongside a smile of smaller triumph. Another day done. Everyone made it.

My students spin around the stairwell and out of the wobbly door. Yelling thanks, they vanish to their soggy slime fish and chip lunch. Even Dean leaves on time to avoid a rubber dinner. Turning the key in the lock, my classroom carnage can wait until I have had a coffee. And a much needed wee. I can hear voices in the corridor. I haven't seen Anna or Liz yet. Turning the corner, I see them. They are standing outside the IT classroom. Something isn't right. Head bowed, Liz is talking through the inspection panel. Anna is hovering. As I approach, she holds her finger to her mouth. Say nothing. A calmer voice than Liz's speaks from the other side. He tells us his name and that he is not coming out. And we weren't coming in.

I call it. 'Assistance required in Education. We have a barricade in Room 8.'

As I run from the door, I can hear the sound of smashing glass. The windows have gone. My colleague Bill meets me at the unit door. His taut face was first out after my callout. Closely followed by my work family. Everyone is on the landing. Moved aside as three burly officers with shields rush through. They throw themselves at the door. It doesn't budge. Not even an inch. Or a centimetre if you're younger than me.

'Is everyone OK?'

'Is everyone here?'

'Yes.'

'No.'

'Where's Jill?'

'Where should she be?'

'I saw her outside the IT room a while back.'

Several call outs on the radio. No answer.

'Don't say it.'

'Is he on his own?'

'Why isn't she answering?'

'Christ. Is she in there with him?'

From whispering to locked out to hostage situation.

Senior officers arrive. They take command. Take a roll call. The fire log is our register. All present and correct. Wrong. Not Jill.

We can hear glass breaking, and yelling. He is on the flat roof. Running around the building trying to get into other classrooms. Shit. Did I close mine? Sick swirls. We are moved downstairs. Officers take control of our unit. We are asked to stay still. Stand fast. Slowly. Realising. This. Place. Isn't. Safe.

Missiles fly past the windows. Anything he can find on the roof. He wants to be moved. He isn't coming down. We aren't going anywhere.

Jill skips in through the side door.

'Helloooo.'

'Where the fuck have you been?'

'Oh. I switched my radio off. Been chatting to the industries tutors. Thought I'd come back for lunch.'

She didn't last her probation period.

Like a lost child, I hug her with relief then go tiger-mum mad. Exploding with fury at the worry she has caused, the realisation of the danger we put ourselves in every day.

We sit in the bowels of the paints rooms, a network of smaller test rooms painted in various shades of mustard yellow or ironic prison sky blue. Pacing round in circles. Churning. Retching back thoughts and fears. There will be no lessons this afternoon.

We're under siege. The prison officers are unimpressed. Our leaders are all on a course. With no one at the helm, we are lost at sea. And we have been well and truly scuppered. They organise national responders when negotiations fail. We're given thirty seconds to grab car keys. Anything else has to be left behind. Grab what you need to get out, but only if it is nearby. Escorted by an officer up the stairs. Our captor is still on the roof. Once he is at the back of the building, we run out, bags above heads in protection mode. Passed like parcels between officers on our route away. Between bricks and a stray toilet seat. And out. Through the gates to stop, breathless, at the reception. As I give in my radio, I can hear orders flying faster than the bricks. Then silence as I switch off the voices. They continue in my head as I give in my keys and am spat out by the airlock, leaving Dean to watch me leave him again.

There she goes, running in them boots. I can see them all running and count them out. Makes a change for me to take a roll call. They are all OK. The ones who are my friends. Not those other men. False friends, they are. All of them. Always taking the piss and trying to get me to snap. Make no mistake, the old me is still there if he is needed, ready to rise, ready to go, just waiting. For now, I will sit inside my room, my domain, my sanctuary. I have all I need here: Kate's books, blagged sweets from Anna, paper and pens from Liz. I look at the artwork and think about what I am going to do when I get out, away from the nosey ones and the ones who call me a grass. Let them say what they want. I can watch them falling into a pit while I fly higher and higher. Like the angels and the smoke. Swirling and free. Over the wall and out of the door. Past the vans, cars, and into the world, reborn.

Walking to the car park, I don't know what to do. I don't. No. I don't want to go home yet. I need to process what has happened. What is still happening to those inside. What they are left with as we are sent home safely. They are colleagues. Friends. I put one clumpy boot in front of the other, focusing on the flowers that cling to my ankles. Holding on by the slimmest of tendrils. I'm parked next to Anna. Her experience tells us this is not normal. Even further from normal than usual. So now what? We congregate at her house. Huddled in a corner, we have what looks like a quiet drink. Heavy coffee cups stop the shaking a little. We talk it through. Then don't talk about it. Leave it to float above our heads. Like the man still on the roof. We laugh about other times. About how glad we are that no students were left in the building. Dean was back in his cell, painting. Paul was writing stories. Adam was long gone. Dave was having a coffee on the spur landing. That it could have been so much worse. Fucking Jill. Fucking hell.

That time. Just joking and laughing. Decompressing. It was so needed. When I get home, I park the car and the day at the door.

'How was your day, Mummy?'

'Bit different. I'm back now.'

'Any kick-offs?'

'Yes.'

'Is it still standing?'

'We shall see.'

'Are you going back?'

'Of course.'

7.

Nine months in and I had emerged a different person. Gasps of air, surrounded by masks, pushing through the fear, and someone else emerged. Clotted sweat head and sometimes silently screaming, but here. Still. Wearing dresses and leggings even in summer. Bright colours to be seen around the estate. Neither grey, nor black and white. Reminding them I am a civilian prison worker. In the space in between. Trusted by no one. Removing the dress belt. Becoming a suicide risk. Double bulges prompting laughs. Swapping secret messages inside bangles with Anna: 'Keep Fucking Going', 'I am enough.' Enough what? Prickling fear? Paper-thin hope? No necklaces allowed. Even the earpiece was risky. Untangling it quick enough to get to the toilet in a fifteen-second break. Being grabbed from behind with it. Or as a potential ligature for another. Trying not to choke myself with the possibilities, it was tucked through tops and sleeves. A cheap magician's trick. Stage directions in my ear. *'Assistance required. E Wing. Code Red.'* I still hear colours. Only in one ear. Not out of the other. It is still holding the screams which might turn to a duller tinnitus drone.

Small bag stuffed into a locker. All personal items removed. No purse, make-up, or phone. No driving licence or bank card to identify me. All I brought in of my outer self were my tattoos. A new £10 note now hidden in the car in case I ran low on petrol when it's my turn to drive. Radio clicks out as I reach the staff room. A short break from the voices. Others are in, shouts bouncing round the tatty chairs from under coats and well-worn hearts. Cradling a coffee, we hear of the incidents since the previous day's dawning. Some we knew through whispers and fractured alerts. Others happened in the noisy nights. Drugs seized, parcels, dangerous strains of Spice to watch for, attacks expected. It's canteen day. The day when debts are paid up, doubled, or sold out. Watch for any unlikely sudden friendships. Which was every friendship here. We were all thrown together into a grey melting pot. New family of disparate, desperate beings trying to hold on as everything else fell away. Hold it together. Hold up others. Hold some close. Hold some at arm's length. I wouldn't touch him with yours, mate.

Alarms sounding. Running. As they run, more appear. Then silence. Now everyone's radio is on. '*Code Red. Barricade in the wing laundry. Late canteen.*' Water flows out under the gate as a tide of shields pushes in. They are a ten-metre world away. Windows punched out. Missiles next. Then a man carried by each corner facing the ground. An officer walks beside. They march past to the seg. As we turn from the window, our men are already spilling into the unit.

Dean grins a wide-eyed 'Morning'. He grabs the dictionaries from the windowsill and sets the room out as the others sludge in.

'Was you hoping for the day off? No offence though, Kate.'

'Did you see that swing?'

'Shouldn't cut the queue.'

'Still, man.'

'He is now. Smashed in proper.'

'Which pad?'

'Say nothing.'

'Safe.'

Another incident, an assault gone by silently under the radar of radio clearance. Not even worth mentioning. A man is stapled up on site. A typical prison diet of blood debt transfusion. And now we are already halfway through the lesson. Miss out the break-out exercises and games, and we will have an issue. So we begin the routine. They run it, like clockwork. Handout: a grammar sheet masquerading as a game. Test each other on spelling. Write a letter of complaint to a slum landlord. Discuss their chances of being homeless on release. Eighty percent of people on the streets have come straight from prison. They talk tactics.

'You got somewhere, Dean?'

'Yeah. Sorted a place till art college.'

'Sam, you good?'

'Nothing doing. Lost me flat three months in.'

'Catch 22 sorting something?'

'They've got a week. Not bloody likely.'

'Do something bad.'

'Not too bad like.'

'Not register bad.'

'Just bad enough to get a hostel bed.'

'Be surrounded by addicts and nonces, though.'

'Maybe not.'

'Get back home.'

'Get back.'

'If there is anything to get back to, Miss.'

'My mum is sorting me a car. Probably stay with her for a few weeks. Just till she's OK for me to leave.'

Pause. Airlock.

And there's the thing. Going back to family means being back where you are known. Who you know. What you know to survive. Don't criticise anyone's choices until you know what their choices are. Starve or find family. Feel protected or be a target. Carry or be carried out in a box. They argue their socioeconomic situation well – enough to pass the listening and speaking exam. Sentences of life learning, words of community spirit and being marked. Some wear the barcodes of belonging. Scan the room. Bleep. Unidentified item in bagging area. White woman. Northern. Seek assistance. Request the price. Reduced shelf-life on all products.

Forty-seven if you live on the streets. My age now.

Twenty if you are found on the wrong one. Theirs.

I've listened. They've spoken. We're now speechless. Now what.

'Miss?'

'Yes?'

'Want to ask you a ting.'

'If I can answer it, I will.'

'How do I . . .'

'Go on?'

'Yeah that. And . . .'

Silence.

'Be a mentor? I mean with a record, like.'

'I can help you find a relevant charity – like Unlock, or Through the Gate, or Remploy. Your experience is really valuable, for other men to see a role model who has been where they are. I'll bring in some job adverts if you like. When are you out?'

'Back on road next month.'

'Well, let's get you on a different track, then.'

'See what you did there, Miss. Probably not worth it.'

'Well, let me be the judge of that.'

'You said you ain't a judge.'

Wry smile. Grin spreading.

'Just kiddin'. See you tomorrow. Safe.'

'See you next time.'

And he strolls off through the door barely hanging on its

hinges. He turns and gently closes it. Then leaps on a friend walking past and is carried back, legs dangling, to the wing.

Lift sharing still helps to laugh away the events of the day. I see a few new faces crying in their cars before we drive away. They appear in the smeared rear-view mirror. By the roundabout, we are all trying to smile. An average day, maybe three alarms and a normal regime, brings talk of the incident. Who, how, where, and why. Anyone we know directly. It flows into news of a boomerang student. I was hailed by him last week like an episode of *Long Lost Family*. Back inside in less than four months with a new addiction and fewer family members to visit him. On tougher days, words of life and family untangle lessons laced in loss.

The journey home is easier with John's affable conversation. His ability to seemingly forget everything as soon as the gate shuts behind us. Another lie of course. What we both don't say is that it keeps me going in. Between weeks of bloody self-harm and weekends of struggling through memory-laden rubbish I can't quite just throw away. I had to take him to the job he loved and he made me fall out of bed, scraping boots and toast too early into the car.

'What is a proper English breakfast?'

'Eggs, sausage, bacon, hash browns, tomatoes, toast, beans, mushrooms.'

'What type of eggs?'

'Fried.'

'Of course.'

'Maybe black pudding.'

'Stop the car. Not sure we can be friends anymore.'

'I'll let it pass this once. If we can also have fried bread.'

'What would you rather have: dicks for fingers or vaginas for ears?'

'Is that your class opener?'

'Totally. Stop avoiding the question.'

'Dicks for fingers.'

'Full marks. See you tomorrow morning at sparrow's fart o'clock.'

This is what prison does. It puts the most random people together in a small, confined space and watch what happens. Locked in. Forced to find connections or fail to survive.

In a radio click I am back in the room. Sharp breaths of morning, mourning the loss of sleep. Chamber of fumes starts me to a half-life. Move a belt hole up an inch every month. Pull yourself together as you slowly disappear before their eyes. Push it back. Hold back and hold out for the end of each day to begin again unscathed. But don't hold, don't touch, or enfold. Never unfold, fragile origami paperskin. Lines written across forehead. Furrows of determined fury. Marks stretched silver, pulled apart in the making of others. Red remembrance of severed bloodlines held in tattoos. An unspoken body of work hiding in plain sight. Because if I stop and think, then I will stop. Altogether, but far from in one place. Parts of me elsewhere. Heart with another, hands encircling my waist, head in the North, everything else gone south.

I arrange the plants along the windowsill, leaves slowly falling with each class. It's a feeble excuse to hug the radiator, bleeding heat into the cold corners of my body. I haven't spoken to another human outside of prison family since yesterday. Holding on to the sadness until set-free-day Friday. Falling asleep fully clothed on the sofa again. Night-waking, walking tilted-hipped to the fridge for food. Chilled air unnoticed. Close the door. Seal shut the leftovers. Pretend we will be able to resurrect them later. False hope fed promises. Start again. Let go.

'Release for Labour and Education.'

Here they all are. Today I have a different peer mentor. His pale face looked greyer, competing with the grey sweatshirt for ashen anonymity. The will to stay hidden in the plain-sight shadows. He quickly pushes the cuffs over a white flash of thick cotton sock. He sees that I see, but neither of us speak. I pull the cardigan over my hand brace. Today's lesson will bear the marks of us all.

'OK, let's start.'

'Miss, you startin' something again?'

'Just the lesson. As always. Must we do this dance every day?'

'All part of the game. You know the rules.'

Except I don't. Hot flush. Cardigan thrown up and off, hanging pelt-like on the back of my chair.

Marker squeals in despair across the whiteboard. Heading: Writing Articles.

'Miss.'

'Any chance we could get some work done today?'

'Your arms . . .'

'What about them?' All the better to signal for help. Drowning under waves of murmurs. 'Yes . . . ?'

'That's not on.'

'What isn't?' Can't I have arms now? How will I stop myself from fraying at the edges? 'Keep your eyes on your work.'

'No, Miss. Your arms. Those marks.'

I'd taken my cardigan off to try and reduce the red flares. Why does the menopause think this is the place to declare itself? In a place full of men on pause.

Under the festival bracelets, a tide of green blue sprays over my skin.

'How did you get them?'

'Don't be lying now. We know.'

Sudden drop of pennies mingle with the glass of light bulb moments. Shit.

'It's not what you think. Honestly.'

'Walk into a door, did you? It's not on.'

'No, really. It was Archie—'

'Don't care what your husband's called. He can't push a woman around.'

'No.'

Louder protests.

'Archie is a black—'

'Don't care what colour he is, Miss. Man shouldn't hit a woman.'

'For fuck's sake will you let me finish?'

'No, Miss. Give us his deets and we'll sort him out for you. On us, like.'

'Christ on a bike. Can I finish?'

'Them marks are domestic. Cowards grabbing woman where it don't show.'

Right. But not correct here. 'Archie is my black Labrador. All forty kgs of him leapt on me last week. That's how I got the bruises.'

And I hold out my arms in appeal. Look at the purple, blue, and green clusters of padprints. Groups of four to a paw, not a hand. Honestly.

'If you're sure, Miss. Because you only need give us the word.'

'The only word you can have is "thanks". For noticing and asking.'

And slowly, in the corner of my eye, another pale face draws back his cuffs to show a cut-off sports sock on his wrist.

'OK. So now look at the sample question and template. See how far you can get writing the introduction. So you all know what you're doing?' Except me. I'm still thinking about the red wrists until the mercy of break arrives.

The grey tide washes out of the room. Normally I make a dash to the loo and photocopier. Not today. Spider senses are tingling. That prickling back of the neck feeling. The one that won't let numbness take over.

'Wait a minute, Josh. I'm not prying. But are you OK? Stupid question. I'm good at them.'

'Actually, I'm not. Can I show you?'

'Before you do, know that I may need to tell someone else. To get you some help. More than I can give.' Just listen to what I squirm to hear. Just be here. Right now. Right place, every time.

'That's OK. I cut myself again. It won't stop.'

As he peeled back the makeshift bandage, blood trickled out past the black clot. Red words of despair and sadness running unedited.

'My Dad's dying. I can't see him. I'll be the man of the house. But there is no house to go back to.'

I'm falling, lurching back to the house stuffed full of everything he couldn't bear to part with. The things that told of where we came from. The letters, old colouring books, accounts, hoarded food, greetings card goodbyes. They'd left him, too. To hold on, he held on to all that remained. Leaving me with the fallout, sliding over into the small patches of space pooled around my feet.

'I'm sorry. I know there are no words to make it better. Put your hand over your wrist. Keep pressure on. I know that's the last thing you want to do, but please. Try. For me, if not for you.'

'If I hold it down, it won't release the pain, Miss.'

Shit. I don't have any gloves, so I hold his arm and press down on the sleeve of his regulation sweatshirt. We're trained to ask them to hold the wound themselves. Partly to stop the transmission of infectious diseases and partly for grounding them. Hold it together, Kate. Hold him together.

'We can get you another later if it comes through.' Another cover-up. 'I need to fetch someone. Or at least some clean pads. I am still listening, but can you take over? Come into the unit with me.'

'Stopped now. Normally does. Hard to find new places you see. Need to get back for lunch.'

Especially when you've been here for years. And in this in-between place, inside and outside the normal world for nearly six. Each day has been marked by a line scratched on the wall of his arms. Higher up there are round cigarette moon scars. 'That's from when we could still smoke.'

The main door below the classroom smacks open and learners pour out, scurrying back for lunch before bang-up. I've scavenged a couple of dressings from the scant first aid kit and we leave the unit together.

'Can I come with you? Let someone know what is happening? You could pick an officer you trust?'

'OK. There's Miss E. She's alright.'

We wander beside the still burnt-out wreckage of the wing lost months back. Black roof trusses. Old barbed wire of no-man's-land. The rooks swoop around our heads as we loiter, holding back from the funnelling of men through the metal doorway. Once it has clanged shut, we make our way to the office. It's lunchtime. The worst time to be there. Throngs of hangry men complaining about the food being not enough, too few chips, too soggy, too hard, too little time. No time to get a shower. All the time to be back behind the door. Rabble voices of simmering rage or resignation. One of the quieter wings for vulnerable prisoners.

As they scurry back to their cells, he joins the queue for lunch, patched up. In the office I explain he is self-harming again. He knows we are opening a casebook for him. I thought he might refuse as it means being woken during the night to check he is still alive. It means facing the door to be seen breathing. He now has the orange folder. He will be on thirty-minute obs and will see the mental health team as soon as possible. As I leave him behind the mustard yellow door, he smiles. A thin smile to just fill the narrow vertical window, another slit to add to his name.

I don't like leaving him there, but he is in good hands. Hands not his own. Or mine. That's the first time I have had to touch someone in weeks. Human contact. No protective space, only connection. Holding him together. Tomorrow will be better. No being kept behind for lines. I must not think. I must not cry. I must not look away. I must not look away. I. Must. Not. Look. Away.

I gain a few more bruises to explain the next day as I bang the heavy gate shut behind me. Leaving the wing, I still carry him with me. This is why I need boundaries. To hold back the tide. The flood of memories. Of knowing what it feels like to be locked behind a mustard yellow, moulding 1970s door. Of living to a regime of meals and timings and not being able to shower every day. For me it was a bath, once a week. Of finding pleasure in small things. Of make do and mend. The guilt of leaving others behind. I must not remember. Put myself together. Re-member heart and head. Be resilient. Sentient. Silent.

I need to find a way through. To not leave with these things in my head. Especially when I am driving home. I already have one speeding fine, which I had to declare to the Governor. Welcome to the club. It's all about the decompression. Release the pressure. But then the blood flows out. Think of something else. Walk back slowly and refocus. And there, sauntering through the grounds with his bag slung on his back, is my answer.

Dean laughs loudly.

'Let you out for good behaviour?'

'Something like that. Been on the VP wing.'

'Nah. That's not my kind of place.'

We walk back to his wing. I am in a bigger hurry than he is. We both know I will have to lock him behind the gate, doing the familiar dance again. I can see his narrow vertical window piled high with oranges from afar. I know this manboy's inner thoughts and loves, yet I am still not sure if he is on a health kick or brewing hooch. I announce our arrival and sidestep the pools of watery pee by the gate.

'Wouldn't you like to be on the enhanced wing? You've earned it.'

'Nah. Glad I'm on my wing.'

'Don't you want more time outside?'

'Too busy painting to look up. Walls are the same anyways.'

'I guess. But on G Wing, you can have your own door key and it would be quieter.'

'Nah. I like the noise outside. Find it calming. More like normal. Plus the lads would miss me. My door is always open anyways. Like a listener.'

'Have you done the Samaritans' training?'

'No chance. I'm not a grass. Keep my thoughts and myself to myself.'

'Probably a good plan. Don't keep it all inside if it's too much. Find a safe outlet.'

'I've got my drawings, paintings, and stories. And the gym every day. Reps are building up nicely.'

'That's body and mind covered. Paper is a good listener, too. Holds more than meets the eye.'

'You been writing again yet?'

'A little. Not a huge amount of time really. Still clearing Dad's house and things keep upending me. I think if I start writing, I might not stop. Home truths.'

'Hang in there. Write it all out.'

'That's my line, Dean.'

We both smile. We're at the main gate now. Dean ducks into the space between wings. It's now decorated in bright stars and rainbows. His marks like cave paintings running along tunnels between a rock D Wing and the hard place H Wing. The place he chose to dream in. They still bear the marks of his histories and futures. He painted words of hope in the airlock between gates. Bright stars and fluorescent graffiti swirls. Banksy rats scuttled along the gaps where there should be skirting boards. These held pens and plastic hearts, taking them into the wings with the self-isolators. I did the same later after my wingman had left. I can't follow him in. There's an incident brewing in the prickly thick air. An officer waves him through the last gate. As I turn the alarms are already sounding.

I learnt to find a good thing, one positive, to leave with each day. Not quite gratitudes. The whole 'find three things that made you smile today' can fuck right off. I need a ton of meds and therapy. Both would come later. I would check in on vulnerable men, write poems with students past and present, speak to officers. Find the reasons why I was there apart from the slowly diminishing pile of family life, an ever-decreasing brown circle on the armchair. The reasons to smile. A chat with a student who was song writing to block out the night-yelling in the next cell along. Seeing a father reconnect with his family through letters. Writing eulogies to be present whilst absent. Group poems in smelly classrooms or chicken runs. Sitting next to Dave as he worked through his whirling thoughts. Writing apps for medical appointments. Checking that the ones I knew were OK. Trying to ignore the muttered 'Snowflake' comments as black and whites go past.

Operation Snowflake was rewarded with yells, shouts, and

the occasional smile on the wing. It didn't matter which. They still had breath in their lungs, voices to be heard across metal landings and grass verges. It was tested a few times. Brought in for questioning, interviewed under cautious warnings, and charged with attempted acts of kindness. Even when it meant defending a prisoner over my new boss. I had an upgraded seat on the landing, witnessing an act of aggression against a prisoner. First class mistake. The man sat in my classroom, a place of safety, whilst officers asked what should happen next. They were fair. Clear and measured. Restorative justice in action. Grudges against me from officers would appear later. But I was in a better position to deal with them. Even as a woman in a male prison. For once, I was the privileged one. The one with keys. Unlocked eyes and common-sense loyalties. Not the political animal that would survive the revolving door of the management office. Just keeping my head high, able to meet eyes across cells and custody suites. Even if night-fractured sleep seeped into my bones. Energy carried away by the rooks each morning as they lined up, the usual suspects.

This morning will be different. It's a Thursday, the last full teaching day of the week. I take over the library on Fridays by choice. Reading groups, creative workshops, often both. We are working on short stories. Settings of familiar and afar. Lords, spies, and workers inhabit the space. They laugh, run, struggle, love, and lose. And begin again each week. That is my gift to myself. To end the week with hope and words. Silences and calm. Imagination and reality. But for now, it's the mechanics of functional skills. How to write a report. I put out the photocopies of an article on the 'Sugar Tax'. How energy drinks will cost even more than they do inside. I can't bring in bags of sugar to demonstrate just how much is in a can of Coke. Any white powder is currency. I have labels to look at instead. I need to embed maths and IT and PSD and British Values and differentiate across a range of learning needs. Today I'm building a wobbly bridge between reading ages of six and two university graduates. And I'm not even allowed any string or straws in class.

I push the windows open before the bar pushes them back to a narrow gap. The air is heavy today. Perhaps a change in the season. Winter is coming. Breathe in. The weight sits on my chest. Hold it in. Close my eyes. Push it out slowly. That's not the door squeaking. Inhaler puffs tiny trails of smoke past my cheeks. Hide it in my belt pocket. I'm carrying a small pressurised canister of steroids. It might backfire. Explode and disappear into thin air. No Dean yet, but I can hear footsteps on the stairs. Still early.

A man appears, grinning, in the doorway.

'Hello, Miss.'

'Morning. You're keen! You're not even one of my students.'

'I have an appointment.'

He waves a movement slip. A paper pass to allow him off his wing. It's signed with a squiggle. Correct date and time. A

Catch 22 appointment. To arrange a bank account, pay court fines, or discuss housing. Or lack of.

He leans on the door frame. He's blocking it. I glance across the landing. Emma is in her classroom opposite, preparing for induction. A heady standard mix of angry newcomers, old safe hands, and terrified first-timers. She is hovering at her door. We exchange knowing looks. Her eyebrow is raised as another man comes up the stairs and loiters at the railings.

'Can I help you?'

'No, Miss. I'm beyond that.'

We look at each other again.

'Release for Labour and Education.'

More men tumble up the stairs. None of mine are in yet. Emma steps back into her classroom. The second man follows her. He puts his arm against the door frame, Del-Boy-bar style. He winks at the man at my door.

I go to my desk and arrange the papers. Arrange them on edge. Pull myself together. Because the air doesn't fill my lungs, no matter how deeply I breathe. Despite the inhaler gulped as I turned away. He's between me and the door. And he has a lookout on the landing. Next to my friend. My sister-in-arms is also potentially trapped. I try to focus on the windows. Look beyond the room to the mist green horizon. Squint to see where the trouble is brewing. Because I can feel it in my bone-tired body. I perch on the edge of the desk ready to try and make a break for it. Push it back. Bile and burning stomach swirls. Push it back. Keep pushing the fire down to kindle hidden resources. I can still see Emma in the corner of my eye. She is hovering. Waiting for the jump. Hand on radio. But hers is already flashing.

As more men come up the stairs, trouble is coming. It's already here. There are now about thirty men between our doors and the exit. And none of them are coming into class. None of them are mine. They are all strangers. Milling about. There's trouble 't mill, my dad would say. And what would he say about this? I can see his sea monster green eyes getting wider as he breathes in sharply. Breathe. Keep breathing. Stop the squeezing clenched fist around my lungs from tightening. Not today, lung disease. Please not today. Not here. In the space in between inside and out. There and here.

The pool of men suddenly spirals. Chaos masks precision tactics as orders are yelled over the screams. A chair flies past my door onto the stairs. Emma screams. The air is spinning. A man is cornered on the stairs. He cowers. Curled up with nothing to protect him. Hands above his head. No surrender is accepted. No Geneva Convention here. He is pelted with chairs, glass bottles. Shards stutter across the hard floor into my classroom. I want to get to him but I can't. The protectors on point warn us back.

'Stand back, Miss. We've got this.' In unison.

They push us back, as chairs bounce off walls. Another streaks past my face. Missiles more lethal as they hit the tiled floors. Sparking upwards in every direction but away. Flint shards backfire into the throng of men. A single man at the epicentre of the tornado. We are definitely not in Kansas anymore.

'Assistance required. Education. Fight in progress.'

'Assistance required in Education. I repeat. Assistance in Education.'

'*Standing by.*'

Looking on. Powerless. Black and whites stream into the building. Our colleagues watch from behind their own safely locked door. Ordered to stand back. Squashed noses on the doors. Family outing curtailed as it rains missiles. Straining to get to us across the riot. The front door smashes through. Greys whirl and spill out of the unit. Marshalled into the foyer. Organised into lines. Only students are left. My protector has gone. So has Emma's.

Dean scurries in.

'You OK, Kate?'

'Kind of. You?'

'Nah. You know me. Sorted, innit.'

'Emma OK?'

'Yes.'

'Not happy about that all going off here.'

Dean checks in on us and starts to clear up the glass. The blood is left for the specialist cleaners who get paid extra to wipe up bodily fluids. A perk to spray bleach on claret covered walls and rails. Derailed the morning's plans by half an hour.

Ten minutes after the screaming has stopped, we are back in class. No time off. No debrief. Everyone is present. I'm incorrect. Not right. No break. Carrying on as normal.

'How do we write an introduction?'

'How do food labels hide the real figures of sugar and salt levels?'

'Can we work out how much is in the bottle of Coke?'

'How will the price change after the "Sugar Tax" is brought in?'

'How might the size change if the price stays the same?'

What has to change? Will I stay the same? I'm going through the motions for everyone's sake. I've played this part before. Kept a level voice whilst being abused by a stalker who didn't like my reporting him. He'd been shown the confidential report. Again, the men had stood up. Put him in the frame. Asked him to stand back.

'But there's 500ml in a bottle, Miss. So I need to double the amounts?'

'Yes. Yes you do. See? We can do maths too.'

'Shouldn't that be math?'

'Yes. Where do you want me to put the apostrophe?'

'S'all right, Miss. You can keep it. One thing at a time, eh.'

'Miss.'

'Yes?'

'Someone at the door.'

Two officers stride in. A torn envelope with coded letters and numbers scrawled on the corner in tow.

'May we have a word, Miss?'

'Outside?'

'I can't leave the class.'

'You have to. This won't wait.'

I trudge out, glad to have a mentor to leave with the class. Leaving them is still a sackable offence. But today all the rules have gone out of the chair-shaped hole in the window.

The officers ask about the fight. They have scrawled three names on the back of the envelope. They tell me in hushed tones that knives were used in the attack. They ask who is in my class. They have the list of names already. Then it registers. One of them still has a knife. Not a homemade shank. But a proper knife, a weapon in my class. But the description they have doesn't match anyone currently bowed over a report on the health risks of obesity. And there's nothing they can do.

And like that, they leave. And I go back in.

And we finish the reports and even manage a practice discussion on prison food. Most of them enjoy porridge. Longer energy levels to push through the day. Or plaster the holes in the walls.

'See you next week, Miss.'

'Take care, Miss.'

'And you. I'll see some of you tomorrow for creative writing?'

'Yes you will.'

'Safe.'

They've tidied away the files, which have to stay in the room. Too much metal to take back to a cell. More weapons in class. I've live-marked the work. Now it should be time to fill in all the context statements: any personal issues, strategies, and notes on progress.

But I walk out of the door and lock it behind me. I meet Emma on the landing. The no-man's-land between our rooms. Barricades and broken glass have gone. Just barbed air. Baited with gasps. We are OK. Of course. Why wouldn't we be? Held back from moving. To tears. Hold back until home time. They had no choice but to leave us in classrooms knowing, suspecting, there were knives still hidden up sleeves and behind books. The pen is mightier than the sword. But I'd rather not test that out.

'Time. For. Coffee.'

'Perhaps we can sneak to S Wing and get some Valium.'

On a knife's edge. Interviewed by our boss. He talks us through it. Offers wisdom and words of support. But it's already buried to rise again later at a crowded gig. Mosh pit screams and delightful fear. Push it back.

Glass crunches like cockroaches under my heels. Tougher than my old boots. Thick skin sliced. Toes curled around the edges. Stop to empty my boots. Go on. Take the piss out of my day's stumbling end. Fill your boots as I walk past the last block before the gate.

'Night, Miss.'

'See you tomorrow.'

'Pass me the ketchup.'

A string swung between windows. Bottle inched across. Primitive telephone lines. Your connection has not been lost.

'Don't drop it. It's already a mess under me window. Stig of the Dump, me.'

'Nah. Roald Dahl's was better.'

'Fuckin' brilliant.'

'Gutted when he died.'

'Totally.'

That reminds me. It'll be time for the Reading Ahead challenge soon.

Click my radio off. Peel out the earpiece. Whirring ear and whining headache. Keys in. Airlock takes my breath away. Rooks commemorate my leaving with a flypast. No more bombshells for today. Think about how close we were. Ketchup splodges. Code Red. Bloody hell. Walking on glass, my feet are sliver still bleeding.

8.

Days blur into one mangled mess of glimpses of light and static tension. We're going nowhere fast. Doze or drive to work. Watch the sunrise and welcome dragonbreath days before entering the gates. Put on a belt. Belt up. Don't speak of what we have left behind. Don't breathe. Smile if you have to. Edge between the lines. Don't move. Walk past the strange-wallpapered corridor with birds stuck to twig trees. Suspended in time. Jail birds. Laugh at the nob someone on the staff roll has drawn on the branches. Collect keys. Get the best set, which isn't worn to failure. Shut the door before flushed face overcomes pale morning. Collect radio. Check the battery. Leave my tally in its place. They know where I am. Check the alert status level. Is it ever not exceptional?

Through the gates and into the estate. Ducks patrol their enclosure. Pacing until their breakfast is scattered across the floor. Feeding time at the zoo. Past the portacabins for adjudications. Rooks hold court on the roof before flying to the tangled sinking skeleton of the burnt-out wing. Still there after two years and counting the cost. It outlasted me. Ribs spread out. Heart stopped. Anaesthesia bones. Numb stasis choking on asbestos air. Last gasps before flatlining. No one wants to call it. Stuck between not being able to afford to leave and the dangers of staying. Put up a new skin of iron to mask the insides.

Today will be just like the last and different to tomorrow. Kettle clicks on before my radio now. I can feel things without having to hear the reports. Reassemble the photocopier before killing a few trees in handouts. This can't be sustained. No internet in the classroom and no USB allowed. No screens except the smartboard I am still not clever enough to work fully. We have managed to convert their writing into text. My doctor's handwriting is too chaotic. Failure to recognise. Try again. I am both different and the same here. More grounded, less anxious. More calm, less feeling. More connected, less open. More human, less character. More flashes of light, less gloom.

Others begin to arrive, pushing the core early birds along their seats. We shift to gather them in. Second coffee time. Office door is now open. Prison admin staff are at their desks. A little less banter now. Medication visits are underway outside. A trail of officers guide the line of dawdling men to Health Care. Move to classrooms and set up for the day. No chance of dashing out for a wee or to grab a forgotten document once the men are in. We are all trapped. Some days the toilet door is locked. Most days, there is still no officer in the building. Always a call away, but no presence. Have the presence of mind to remember that. A friend once asked if I taught behind a screen with an officer in the room. Laughable. Even with men convicted of manslaughter. Man's laughter coils up the stairwell. They're here. Time to get this show on the road. Not on road yet.

Dean bursts in with his usual rainbow exuberance. He has had a great night. Painting and not sleeping. His eyes glisten, getting wider by the minute. He brings a picture. His first watercolour. It's a dragonfly over a reed-filled pond. Blues and greens wash over me. It's for me. It is me. He has put the memorial tattoo inscribed on my arm into flight. There she is. Alive and moving through the air on wings of glass. I can hear her shallow breathing. I can see her agate eyes glistening in the sunlight. How did he know? It takes me right back there. Waiting. Holding my breath as hers stops whispering. Hospice black and blue.

'Do you like it?'

'I don't know what to say.'

'Gawd. That isn't like you. You OK?'

'It's beautiful. Thank you. But how . . . ?'

'I see them too.'

'What?'

'The glimpses of darkness.'

He shudder-shakes his curly head of hair, gets back into character and walks away, leaving my jaw-broken heart on the sticky floor. Breezing into the unit to collect the paint for the admin office. I watch his back. If only I could have always done that.

I feel upended for a while. The other, outer world isn't allowed in here. I need the boundaries. To not be where the boxes and chaos and yellowed paper planes are. To leave behind the deceased estate coroner emails. I want to be inside. I'm already only inside my head. The clang of the bruising gates reminds me of where I am. A different world. The essence of what it means to be human. Of what is left when all the masks, costumes, make-up, props, and backdrop cast have left through the visitors' gate. There are some able to stay in a role, typecast. To continue as the kingpin or skittle, the wrecking ball or referee. I can be me without mentioning my name or where I live. My past doesn't count. Just the present. A gift of being here for the moment. One by one. A sign of hope for the men who might be able to leave their deeds behind. Of not being an ex-offender on exit. Of not being relative to what has happened. Of being a human reborn. Only nurture's lessons might overrule nature's desire to leave. To not come back. As I did every day.

I wonder what it might be like to not have to live in the space between worlds. To be constant. Not shifting, dissimilar. Always hiding something. How was my day? Fine. Apart from the fights, propositions, targets, questions, stories, and silences. I've gone from crashing on the sofa to being caught mid car crash. It's safer to stay permanently alert, numb, calm, anxious, prepared, shocked.

I didn't see it then. I didn't see anything after the worst days came in waves dipped in froth foam silver crests.

The day passes uneventfully for me. I report the commotion

outside the wing opposite. Cell numbers outside each window screwed to the wall above the rat poison boxes.

'Kate in Education to any Induction Wing staff.'

'*Go ahead.*'

'Assistance required in cell four. He's either training for an interview at IKEA or he isn't happy. He's having a crisis.'

'*Understood.*' Pause. '*How do you know?*'

'He's taken apart all his furniture and is posting it piece by piece through the narrow vertical window slots onto the scrawny grass outside. He's quite a flat-packer. Be careful.'

'*Standing by.*'

No curtains to draw. No need. No one else in the room has noticed. I think about how they might see what I said. Am I a traitor? A scrawny grass too? Will I be kettled or torn limb from limb and laid out outside, too? I seem to escape unscathed. Another standard morning at the office.

Later I found out he was doing better. Now on a different wing and on bed watch. Probably charged with criminal damage. He would be charged for the replacements from his £5-a-week wages. His family would need to send more money in to support him. He would be assessed up to every fifteen minutes according to his risk level. Day and night. He would be accompanied by the orange folder, an ACCT document. I'd seen too many on the wings. Each one was an individual mental health document, assessing what was needed and how many meaningful interactions with staff a man should have per hour. We were trained and retrained on how to fill them in and support the walking story. A full risk assessment. All conversations, movements and incidents should be recorded verbatim. With times, dated, signed, and initialled twice. State the facts. Nothing but the facts. Because you could be repeating them in a coroner's court if things went wrong. Lives depended on those words. During the night, men would be watched for signs of life. If they were facing the wall, they were woken up. Back stories and progress reports were included. Steps needed for him to come off observation were listed. Triggers and issues were also reviewed. Medication noted. Eye contact. Words. Silences. Movement. No being still allowed. Just progress. When it was my turn to fill the entries, Big Mother was watching you.

I'd swapped my own brood for a gaggle of lost men amidst the sea of one-man crime waves. Blank stares and raised eyebrows. A new staff intake, too. Working on the wing was certainly eye-opening. I'd arrive early, as the men were taking pots of porridge and toast back to their cells. They had to be locked up again before release for work and education. I had a list of men who couldn't leave the wing and needed support. Normally about fourteen, but others could be added after the safeguarding meeting. Some hadn't left their cells for weeks. Living and eating next to a metal toilet.

Working directly for the prison meant I had more information, for worse not better. I knew case histories and index crimes, which I had to file away in the back of my head for much later. How they had been damaged, too. Keep the survivors outside close by. I knew some triggers and issues. Or I discovered them.

'Here she is. Code Snowflake.'

'Thanks Officer Evans. Just you today?'

'Couple out escorting Len to his holiday home again.'

'Not the seg again. What happened this time?'

'Over the railing again. Bouncy castle and everything.'

'I'll go and see him later.'

'You signed in?'

'Always. I've seen the line-up of ACCTs too. Most of the names are in my class. Want me to keep notes and fill them in? They'll be with me all the time anyway, poor sods.'

'That'd be grand. Frees me up for the servery. It's cheese butties again so there's bound to be a reet kick-off.'

'Roll correct?'

'Lee mucked it up by moving. Sorted now. Unlock next.'

'Good. So no need for anyone to get sent to maths lessons, then?'

Unlocking the shabby classroom is next. Peel the ketchup off the tables and scrape the chairs up off the floors to form the spokes of a broken circle. The wheels have already come off. They fall through the gaps and spill into seats one by one. All unseen for a day until they meet each other. A couple of debtors, three on suicide watch, one on crutches, one terminal, one with dementia. All strong beyond their beliefs.

Friends and uneasy bedfellows. Bedraggled. Dressing-gowned. Let's call it a housecoat. At least you're covered. Unlike last time's dingle dangle wait for an officer. Let's take the register. Burnt toast and promises smells waft up the stone steps. Along with other scents of a dirty protest next door and a sugaring on the other side. Nice neighbours.

'Miss!'

I freeze. That's the choice I pick today – between run or freeze. A shit-streaky blue mattress is slid past the classroom door. Brown trail snails past. Shit. I forgot the Vaseline again. There's a smell you don't get rid of quickly. Exhale.

'Yes, I think I will give it a miss, thanks, Dave.'

'See you later, Miss.'

'Missing you already.'

They are slumped into seats this morning. It's been a night of unrest, and burning skin smells sink into the brickwork. The very fabric of this room holds everything closer. Window slits bring a welcome light slice and cut grass fumes.

'Right. Daft question time. How is everyone?'

'Living the dream, Kate.'

'Another day in paradise.'

'So here's a warm up.'

'Nice one miss. We doin' porn today?'

'Like the lesbians on a train story?'

'Nope. No. No way José.'

'Who's José – your new piece?'

'Is it really going to be one of those mornings?'

'Morning glory, you say?'

'Right. Let's start again, shall we? Good morning.'

'Morning, Miss.'

'Today we're going to write a story.'

'Are you fuckin' kidding?'

'No way got the stamina for that.'

'You're only good for a quick tug, eh Smithy?'

'Packed three in this morning. Still horny as fuck.'

'Is there no end to your eloquence?'

'What about my end? Wanna check it out?'

'Put it away. You'll frighten the horses.'

'Let's do some writing.'

Chair scraping sighs slump back.

'Jamie, hand out the pens.'

'Sure thing, Miss. No paper?'

'Just four pieces. One on each table.'

'Rationing back, Kate?'

'Christ, how old do you think I am?'

'Pre-war at least.'

'Jesus Jamie, which war were you thinking?'

'Second world war . . . Falklands . . . Afghanistan?'

'Fair play. You win. So now all you have to do is write one sentence.'

'Makes a change.'

'Normally done for us.'

'But you have to take turns. Pass the paper round.'

'Just one sentence.'

'If you can.'

'Just the one, then.'

'A whole sentence?'

'Up until parole, if you like.'

'OK, Miss. You first.'

'Once upon a stretch.'

'Limo speeding past the red light.'

'Green grass of home no longer.'

'On the run, he's safe.'

'Speeding away from town, she's next to me.'

'Like the last time I saw her.'

'Face made up.'

'Like a car crash, spider eyelashes.'

'Bat out of hell.'

'Mouth wide open, ready.'

'Fire-breathing dragon hoarding gold teeth.'

'Smiling false smiles to trick me.'

'Into the deep dark water.'

'Sinking or swimming to the bank.'

'Robbery gone wrong, blown safe.'

'Say nothing.'

'Say nothing.'

'Kate?'

'Yes?'

'You tricked us again. We've written two things already.'

'So there's a chance you'll write some more, then?'

'You'll be lucky.'

'Well that answers that question, then.'

Words and stories float around the room, pass-the-parcel dreams as we unwrap another layer each time. Bunting stories decorate the tables. The glue that holds us together where all others are banned. We skirt around the inner stories, hold them in ideas and images we pretend aren't true. The speeding car, robbery, beautiful girlfriend, hell that smells of burnt skin and scorched bread. The stories spread onto the spurs, into wing jobs, and fly out of the gate if they are lucky. As straight as the rooks fly, ill-prepared, down the lanes. They often came back to write the sequels.

Of these boomerang men, Dave is admittedly one of my favourites. He's moved from stories stolen in class to a wing cleaner job. Flood of pride met by mop and buckets. Dave has up days and down nights. Silent smiles and glazed tired eyes often meet across the landings. Writing found poems together checks both of us in as safe. As I move around the spurs, he approaches me, giggling. Officers' stern looks.

'Miss. Kate. I think we need to talk.'

'Is this the "it's not you, it's me" talk?'

Black and white eyes are narrowing. Hands on belted radio.

'I need to talk to you about my feelings.'

'Eeerm. OK.'

And then Dave is down on one knee, presenting me with a plastic crystal doorknob by way of a huge diamond ring. We both burst out laughing.

'Will you . . . ?' Of course he never finishes the joke. The gesture is enough.

'I can think of a couple of reasons why not. Your beautiful girlfriend and my husband.'

We are both still sniggering as we go our separate ways across the railing landings. The officers crack a smile. All is OK. Even if the snowflake has melted a little.

The next week sees Dave walk sheepishly up.

'Kate. Miss. I didn't offend you, did I?'

'You made me smile on a shit day. So no. Of course not. But try not to make a habit of it. If someone took it wrong, you could be on a charge and extra time.'

'I've been a bit worried. You know I am loyal to my girl. Did you tell your husband? Am I in trouble?'

Pause. Should I tell Dave? Not? Give something of the other, locked away me? Fuck it. 'I did tell him I now have both a work husband and a wing husband. Sorry, I am two-timing you all.'

He feigns shock.

'And then my real husband said it was OK.'

'Really, Kate?'

'He said because if we were married you would never get any anyway.'

We conspirator grin.

'See you next week, Kate.'

'You will.'

There is no rushing around the landings. Anticipate the worst and hope for the best. The group loitering at the exit wave a welcome. I'll see some of them later for workbooks. Things to keep them occupied. More than that. Things to keep them going. Things to send home. To reconnect. To remember. To remember. To put them back together again. This world without phones or internet. My head is still buffering. But connection has been lost. Please wait. Refresh and check again later.

The wing walking sits uneasily with the conveyor belt classroom in Education. Four weeks was just enough to glimpse the lost and found falling. Sensing a creeping disconnect, our manager sets us all a challenge. He is a genius wrapped in affable manboy attitude. He knows we are all struggling and need something to spark off. We are told to work in small groups to introduce a new teaching method into our lessons. A chance to regroup with Anna, Liz, and Emma. Huddled round cauldrons of coffee we try to grasp brain fog slipping through shaking fingers. Anna drops her pen, scrabbles round for it, and then comes up for air.

'That's it!'

'That's what?'

'That's what we should do. I read an article about it last week.'

'Anna, are you ever off the clock?'

'You know me too well, my friend.'

'After ten years teaching inside, you are practically a lifer.'

'So I saw an article on penless teaching and thought it could work here.'

'Eeerm OK. How does it work?'

'There is a No Pen Day every October, which encourages

147

people to think about other ways of teaching and communicating.'

'That's a new one.' Alongside all the other days like Sign Language Day, Glaucoma Awareness Day, LGBTQI+ Week. We skirted around National Sausage Day.

'It could really open things up. What do you all think?'

'My instinct is that it will be bloody difficult for English. It's so reliant on writing skills. But let's do some research. Could be fun.'

'Exactly. Remember Guy?'

'Who was that?'

'The man who was losing the use of his hands, remember?'

'Oh yes! Hasn't he left now?'

'He was here a few months ago. No sign of being a boomerang boy, which is nice.'

'We wrote poems via spoken words. Could work within the Functional Skills lessons.'

'Same with maths.'

'And induction.'

'So it's a plan. Find the connections between induction, English, maths, and personal development through no-pen lessons. Let's split up and look for clues and meet again next week.'

The gang separates and kintsugi gold trickles back into classrooms ahead of the next grey wave. There are more meetings, reports, plans. These management-led initiative chores knit us back together into a gangster gran's itchy crochet blanket. String tendons holding tired bones in place. Soon it's time to flesh out the plan. Lay sagging skin over the surface to meet the moment.

Dean's already in the building, moving between the classrooms to see what has been planned. As a peer mentor he needs to see how best to support the lessons' outcomes. As a manboy inmate, he will no doubt be strategically darting between rooms to maximise his intake of Post-its, paints, and the odd sweet.

'OK. So remember I said today was going to be a little different?'

'Are we going on a trip, Miss?'

'I'd kill for a McDonald's right about now.'

'At 8.30 a.m.?'

'Hell yeah.'

'Bangin' muffins.' Sniggers.

'Well I'm afraid that isn't going to happen. But we are going penless.'

'What the fuck?'

'As ever, your enthusiasm overwhelms me, Aaron.'

'Fuck yeah!'

Pens catapult across the room, following narrow sightlines I register for later.

Pause.

'Now what?'

'First up, some punctuation.'

'No change there then.'

'No pens doesn't mean no work.'

Dean hands out the paper with an oversized stream of words printed out. A standard breathless volley of ideas for a Monday morning.

'So how the fuck do we sort this mess out?'

'I ask myself that every single day, Lee.'

'No really. What the fuck?'

'So you've noticed there are no commas at all here. Or full stops.'

'Bloody carnage, innit.'

It may well go that way.

'No pens needed. Dean, can you hand out the foam bananas, shrimps, and raisins please?'

Suddenly perky meerkats are in the room.

'We're going to use the bananas as commas, shrimps for apostro— Wait a second . . . Where did the punctuation go?'

Incoming sugar rush. Even Dean has a face like a sack of hammers.

'Right. Let's start over. Shout out what you might need and you will be handed the right markings.'

'OK, Miss.'

No one touches the group sweets. They know the alphabet of Hep A to C is rife inside. And Jack left class last week after declaring his status. He came in with a black eye, cheerily explaining he was hitting himself instead of cutting after testing positive. No fist bumps that day.

'What's next then?'

'Dominoes.'

'Cracking. What's the minimum?'

'You're always looking to do that, Carl.'

'Nah, Miss. I mean cash or canteen.'

'All bets are off.'

'Bollocks.'

'Let's keep them on, eh.'

Now they work as a group to match the word with its partner.

'What's.'

'What is.'

'Couldn't.'

'Could.'

'Could not you prat.'

'Won't.'

'Er. Shit. Wo not?'

'No, dipshit. Will not.'

'I'll knot yours in a minute.'

'Don't.'

'Do not.'

'Shan't.'

'Sh…Shan. Shit. Shane. What d'you reckon?'

'Shall not.'

'Wouldn't.'

'Would.' Giggles. 'Wood . . .'

'Would not, ya eejit.'

'Finished, Miss.'

They've made a string of words, worked round the room, across tables and chairs. We look over the result. Lifer lines linking to a struggling youngster. Caught on a line, they reel him in over the next week. Teach him how to cook in a kettle. Hide sugar. Make a phone call. Not shake hands. One Twix is two come canteen day.

Chairs screech in under wonky tables. Lesson plans and papers already in my bag for next week. Much tidier than my children. Military precision when it comes to lining up resources. Logistics of groupwork. Tactics for engagement. Interchange of advancing, retreat, and surrender each week. PTSD on hold until assessment is complete. Never put 'why, what, how, where, when, which' on the board. That's how you file a report. Log an incident in detail. Flash back and forward chairs, tables, and books. Officer down. Scent of lunch approaching brings him back. Desert of faces, we manoeuvre the conversation to other things. Lights out. Door locked. Damage done. Again. And again. Try again next week. Check in on him later, pretending I need to drop off a set of notes for Sam, who is writing a song. In the event, I get both done. Eyes blue not black. My favourite three little words:

'See you, Miss.'

I see you, too. We are still here. Amidst the wreckage of broken bones, homes, and hopes. Walking off the wing, I leave behind the graffiti-strewn walls commissioned by the prison. Is it just window dressing? Bright colours on steel fences. Compound fractures dressed in rainbows. A thin veneer, or healing skin meshing over fences and barriers? Time to lower mine a little. Go home for the weekend. Perhaps sleep. Never dream. Talk to my kids. Ask them about their week. Any playground proposals? Fights or flounces? When work is home and home isn't working. There's something in the air. The smell of broken bones healed twisted. Racing to standstill. Hearing alarms in shops. Reaching for a radio when the crowded gig surges forward. Push it back. This is not a drill. You don't get second chances at moments of madness. Keep walking. Tilted hips and screaming ears. Until tomorrow. Always tomorrow.

9.

Colin greets me from his chair. Unable to get up, his eyebrow raised at the prospect of a visitor. Suspicious. Angry at being recalled. Clearly seriously ill. His skin is at breaking point, drawn tightly over his skull sunken face.

'Hello. It's Colin isn't it?'

'Says so on the door.'

'I've been asked to come and see you.'

'Why? What do they want with me now? I've done my bird and still got recalled.'

'Nothing like that. Because you're in your room a lot, I wondered if you needed anything.'

'Another room. And a key in the soap, thanks.'

'I left it in my office. So we'll have to go with the standard fare.'

'Which is?'

'We could do some writing, perhaps? Or art? Both, even?'

'Write what exactly?'

He is well-spoken. Older and in self-imposed isolation.

Wary of the ways of the wing. A professor of restorative justice at the university of life. Survivor. Aggressor. Now seeking a chair in mediation, sitting between the outside of last week and the inside of the next forty-eight.

'I have some prompts. Is it OK to sit down?'

'You can have my seat.'

Actually I can't. I have to stay between you and the door. Being taken hostage isn't on my list of jobs for the week. So I sit on the edge of his bed. Like a teenage visitor.

'Here's a poem. Nothing too heavy. Fancy reading it?'

So we read it a couple of times. Shifting from cheek to cheek in awkward measures. Sizing each other up. As ever, I have no idea why he is in prison until I choose to look at his records, if at all, and always after a class. This new work means it's a longer relationship with no nasty surprises at the end. And he has no idea why I would want to work with the likes of him. His words, not mine. That makes us equal, then.

Twenty minutes later, we're writing a poem of our own. This poem is twitchy, new born from old bones. It's self-sabotaging, lifeless, edited. Cut up, strung out, and inspected. And now I'm cut up. He knows it's a metaphor. No mixing with this one.

'Kate?'

'Yes.'

'I've been thinking.'

'About what?'

'Could you get me a plant?'

'I have permission to get some soil, seeds, and a pot from

the industries manager. So, yes I can. We can watch it grow.'

'I just think . . . it would be nice to have something alive in here.'

And he's right. I'm dead inside still. Avoiding the issue. Hiding from the coroner, the funeral director, and the far-flung relatives I'd like to throw further. But he is flickering to life. Peering through the silt, becoming unburied.

'So can I come and see you again?'

'Of course. I'm not going anywhere.'

Except we are. Moving slowly, carefully towards connecting enough to find out why he is isolating. Not because of debt. Not because of threats. He is waiting. For the glasses we have now filled in a request form for. He is waiting to find out if his appeal will be heard. If he has to make the effort to learn the rules of this wing. And for him, it is a huge effort to move across the small cell. I see myself out. Not down. That happens next.

I have another new resident to see. Crossing the estate, I see some familiar faces.

'Let you out again have they, Miss? Isit?'

'Been on holiday?'

'Nope. Worst tan ever if I had.'

'Idiot. Excuse him, Miss. Sorry for your loss.'

'Thank you. We've all lost something haven't we?'

'Too right. Maybe we should write a poem about it!'

'Hold onto that thought. You may regret saying that.'

'Oh fuck. You is active, Miss.'

'Not quite in the way you mean. Have a good day.'

'Another day in paradise.'

'Living the dream.'

Half-awake. Half-aware. Half-life in between a bare cell and a crammed house. A blank page and weighty volumes waiting. Both are pushing me away. Closing in.

'Don't shut the gate, Miss!'

Officers rush past to join the fray. I'm feeling pretty frayed at the edges by the sight of a small grey man struggling underneath so many officers. A lion brought down by zebras. I sigh as he is relieved of the makeshift shank in his hand. He is marched past me to the seg. I can finally go onto the wing.

I'm met by the stench of burnt kettle curry. Brown-ringed steel tubs wait in the servery for collection. There are other smells, which I cannot quite identify. Variants of burnt tea bags, Spice, toast, damp towels, Cornish pasties, disinfectant despair. The wing cleaner is swilling down the lower floor with a bucket of over-powering bleach. He is the only person visible now. Two officers sit in the office. They are going over the records for canteen orders, overpriced crisps, chocolate, deodorant, and toothpaste. They don't look up when I walk in. I sign the visitors' book. Still no dignitaries or film star arrivals, then. I drop my papers on the desk. Here are the envelopes and paper the men have asked for. Now they smile. It will make their job a tiny bit easier. One less question to pile up with the others.

'Afternoon, Miss.'

'You know you're the only ones to not call me Kate anymore, right?'

'Yes, Miss. Who do you want?'

'Well, Tom Hardy would be great. But as he isn't on the unlock list, I will have to see Jim instead.'

'You can't. He's self-isolating.'

'And that's why I want to see him. To see how he is and to give him what you call a distraction pack and what I prefer to see as an engagement pack. Maybe get to speak to him about meeting up each day to begin slow reintegration.'

'You have some?' Tired eyes flicker to life.

'Yes. I brought some spare to leave with you for the weekend.'

'Let's show you to his cell. He won't be leaving anytime soon, though. They all know what he did. What he's in for.'

You're in for it now. Locked behind a door until they decide it's been long enough.

We walk down the upper landing, passing pale blue doors with observation windows. Closed. Everyone is either banged up or at work in the laundry or industries. I have got thirty minutes to see as many of the self-isolating men as I can before they officially go back behind their doors. If they have even come out. Jim has asked to be locked in. I alternate who I see first. I'm taking away their shower time.

The officer crunches the key in the lock and slowly opens the door.

'You dressed, mate? Someone to see you. Shower when you're ready.'

He comes to the door frame, unwilling to cross the line. I reassure him that no one else is out yet. He peers out and quivers back inside. This is one wing where no one is prepared to take any risks. He won't come out. I can't go in. Apart from the stale 1970s Tupperware odour which skulks out, there are other things to consider. He is no danger to me, but it's likely I could get caught in the middle of an attack on him. Particularly as he has been in the news again. Pleading not guilty. No appeal. He has a few redeeming features, though. Despite what he has done. One is his love of reading. So he has joined my unseen book club. They have a few chapters a week to read. Answer questions and ask one of their own. Character motivation, realism, plot twists spill out. Insights which wouldn't be out of place in a graduate seminar. In the university of crime, thoughts and philosophies are scraped up and typed up to pass onto the next man to answer. The beginnings of connection. No introductions. Just faceless words. No tone. No touch. Like texting. But no phones.

We talk about the last chapters and he grabs the next three. Then he scuttles into his brick-lined room and pulls the blanket over his heavy head. Here is the serial book in action. Drip feeding him Dickens as it was written. The man in a cell relishes the slums, courtrooms, and characters. The grim popular style sits well from his vantage point.

I've got a few minutes to see another man on the wing. Luckily, he is out of his cell and walking towards me across the water-pooled floor. He's not waving but drowning. Neil's sleeves are rolled up. He's ready to show me his work for today. I've never seen his tattoos before, and I wonder what the black and red outlines would form as they come into view. The memorial roses are red. And they are bleeding. He's opened up old wounds. Cut the memories out of his head. He's learning to feel again. Pain helps him to feel alive.

I knew he self-harmed. I'd been told beforehand, no pun intended. So the blue gloves were ready in my pocket.

'It's OK, Miss. I'll do it.'

He holds a crumpled piece of blue roll on the worst cut.

'Only a flesh wound, Kate.'

His tattoo was split open. Healed slices and falling petals hung down. I was looking into his thoughts. What had got under his skin.

'I know I can't stop you, but I wish we could find another way for you to feel. To not feel like this.'

'I dunno. I'm doing it proper now. Using a clean blade. Not sharing, either, like you said.'

'It's a start. So, what do you want to happen next? Once we've done the ACCT forms.'

'Nothing. You can't bring her back.'

'I know.'

We sit on the sticky bench surrounded by ketchup stains and pizza crusts. We've got some time before he has to be locked up again. The officers have seen us outside in the open and they know this will be written up as his one meaningful engagement for the next few hours. They can then focus on the others amidst the roll calls, paperwork, orders, complaints, and apps. No shower gel sting today. So we sit. He notices my tattoos. Nods. Sniffs. We say nothing. Officers begin pacing. It's nearly time for him to return. He looks up.

'No date on yours, then?'

'No. Because it feels like every day.'

'It's worse now. Tomorrow. The next day.'

Tomorrow's date is scored under the exploding roses. This is not plucked out of thin air. Heavy air weighs thick. Ten years in the making. Oxygen tanks empty. Ever the English teacher, I notice the font. The curls and details aren't a prison tattoo. This is an older loss. From a time before or between lives.

I want to ask him how he marks the date. But mark isn't the right word. He's cut up and my heart bleeds. Go careful. Think about the words. Notice the silences. The lines and ways of speaking without talking. Words whispered in blood.

'What would help you tomorrow?'

'It can't be done. I've asked.'

'Tell me anyway. Pass the idea to me. Share the weight.'

'I want to visit the chapel. Light a candle.'

'I can understand that. Would writing a letter help? One you can't send.'

'Maybe. Not sure.'

Silence. Waiting. Knowing.

'I need to go back now. Thanks, though.'

He walks back to his cell. Stops. Walks on. Door bangs shut.

I go back after my class, which annoys work husband John because he wants to leave on time. On the other side of the door I wave a piece of paper and envelope at Neil. He nods. I slip it under his door.

Paperwork over. Safeguarding team alerted. I didn't promise anything. There could be a reason why he has been denied the chapel visit. Security reasons. Safety concerns. More paperwork. He is in luck. I know who to ask. Who to email with the question. His chapel visit is arranged. He can be escorted there after lunch. Once everyone who wants to hurt him is in their cell until unlock. He is still in pain. Skin paper cuts smart. Clever candle wax seals the gap for a time. Loss held in hope of future resurrection. Seeing his stillborn daughter again. Her face unclotted and smiling eyes open.

Walking back to the unit, the deputy governor greets me.

'How's it going? Been hearing good things, Kate.'

'That makes a nice change. It's OK, thanks. How are you?'

'I've been thinking.'

'That does sound risky, Simon.'

'Can we have a writing competition for all the wings?'

'What kind of thing are you thinking?'

I've learnt to be guided by what the experts want first and then temper it with some Northern tact. What some might call blunt pragmatism, others just plain rude. Always honest.

'I want to see stories, words, creativity. Something encouraging.'

'The way I'm feeling, we should probably stick to short stories. Shorter the better.'

'Maybe five hundred words?'

'If you'd asked me on Monday, then maybe. But as it's Thursday, I'm thinking more like six.'

'You can't tell a story with only six words.'

'Careful. That sounds like a challenge.'

'Really? Just six words.'

'It isn't wise to challenge me.'

'Why do you say that?'

'Because you're now imagining a story.'

'Hang on a minute . . .'

'Paper's a better friend than people.'

'That's a good one.'

'Slightly altered Anne Frank. But let's do this.'

'What would you need from us?'

'Ah, that's easy.'

'We could find a bit of money.'

'I need two things from you.'

'What? Name them.'

'A story. And an idea for a picture to go with it.'

'A picture?'

'I'm going to print them all out on a picture. To form an exhibition. Include as many human stories as possible. From anywhere and everywhere.'

'I'll leave that with you then.'

'I'll send you an entry form.'

He walks back to his office rubbing his stubble chin. There's a lighter sparkle in his eyes, even if he has learnt to never challenge a Northerner who is given nothing to build stories from. Just a human being in a blank room. Ideas unlocked by the spaces in between words. The quiet waiting. Silence speaks louder behind high fences and barbed wire. The echoes felt for years in flashing pictures and the smell of blood burning.

Burning bridges was one thing I was good at on the outside. After a day's dishragged dragging, I had heated phone calls with estate agents and lawyers as we cleared the house ready for sale. Peeling back the layers of time, each old-found toy and new-found bill cut deeply. Opening up the past and aches driving back home to bed again. Back-breaking work to clear a hoarded house, with layered rooms of sediment and quicksand stories to suck me under. I found my old school books, photos of happy glimpsed holidays. The silt of mouse nests washed over the carpets. Threadbare patience by nightfall. I still had four hours' drive ahead of me to get back to my normal. Nowhere to sleep whilst we cleared it all. Solving nothing but the passing of time. And that was one thing I didn't have on my side.

The presence of loss stretched its thin fingers into the prison. All around me was loss: lost time, family, contact, homes, and hope. But amongst the debris of what remained was the charred promise of new beginnings. Of what might come after. Voids were spaces, silences, pauses before something happened. With luck, the hairs on the back of my neck would rest awhile as Anna and I plotted something. Something big. To find the gaps people had slipped into. To recognise and acknowledge our common humanity. To make a meeting place for staff and men alike.

We wanted to challenge ideas. Emotions that were left to fester and grow into difficult, complex behaviours. Working with men in prison was a high wire act without a net. Would anyone bring out the inflatable crash mat if we were spotted? I honestly thought it was a bouncy castle the first time I had seen it being dragged out. No fun to be had, though. Slid under the railings where a man had climbed over the top. A reaction to bang-up. The reminder of freedom's loss. The choice to challenge authority's fear of losing another man in custody. Dangling on the edge of reasons known to many.

Energy levels were low. Slipping away selves running for cover. Keeping up the levels of vigilance was slowly sapping my reserves. Keeping back the tide of childhood memories when faced with the same mucky mustard doors and pale faces was becoming more difficult. I needed a project other than myself. I was losing. And there it was: loss.

Anna and I went to our manager to ask for his permission to create an exhibition. Anna was like a terrier with a bone when she had a project. A seasoned prison teacher, layered in loss and cardigans, she was part dynamo, part grinch. We had the theme. We knew it was provocative enough to get responses whilst being open to interpretation. We'd both lost things for the better and worse; family sat on both sides of that fence, and I was getting a splintered arse dealing with mine.

The exhibition would include art. Anna had her eye on boosting the morale if not perhaps the morals of a talented, violent man currently in his seg second home. I wanted as many as possible to feel able to write something. Subtitles for emotions. Stories of selves lost in the cracks. It might stop us cracking up or even crack us up. So we began to piece together the edges. How to frame it. Left to us to shape, it became a six-word short story competition, providing the entrants with an example alongside the paper for an entry. Each person would be encouraged to suggest an image to be printed behind the words. Exhibited in the library, we would invite judges to choose winners. Tea, coffee, and cakes would enable us to mingle with the other invited dignitaries.

Entry forms were printed off and circulated to the wings. I approached the staff for their own entries. Raised eyebrows. You're welcome. The subject of loss was a deliberately double-edged sword. But the pen is supposed to be mightier. And the men were stronger still. They told of lost children, miscarriages, family. Stories of lost pasts and new directions. Loss was tempered by gain. Leavings were arrivings. Hide and seek. I was entrusted with a baby scan picture to put with a story. A family photo which was returned the same day to smiles. This was a privilege. Telling a story of what I had gained whilst losing so much of my former self.

'Dear younger me, I'm writing to tell you that it doesn't get better for a long time. Things will get tough and you will get used to losing things and people along the way. I wish I could tell you that it gets easier but it really doesn't. There will be bumps along the way and hurdles for you to face. But you will overcome them all and become a man. You will have dark times and you will do time in prison. You need to cherish your family while you have them as they will get lost as you go on your journey. Try to be brave and strong when others around you are asking you to deliver things for them. You will do it for your family and they will be safe. You don't have any choice but it isn't the right path for you. That will come later. When you become a mentor and guide other men to think better of themselves. In the darkest of places you will be the light that is needed. You will be respected and larger than the life you thought you would have. People will see you as a role model, which is both a responsibility and a curse because you feel the weight of it. But you will have found the strength to carry others when they cannot go on and the thought of them will keep you going when you are down. Because there will be ups and downs until you find your way. Hang in there because it will be worth it. You will lose your freedom but you will find yourself in the process. So for now, keep smiling that smile and don't forget to put that tooth under the pillow for later. You will be OK.'

'Thank you for that opening speech, Callum.'

We are all smiling like the photo of mini-Callum. Rascal beam for his first school photo. His mum has sent it in and wants it put back on the mantelpiece again sharpish. We hold a composite image of him as a found child and man lost from her view.

'I'm Thomas, the peer mentor for the personal and social development courses and your MC for the afternoon.'

Cheers and whoops from the grey men in the audience.

'I want to thank you all for coming today and the college for hosting the Loss Exhibition. Now we will hear from Chris, the education manager.'

'I've written something by way of telling you a little about myself. Despite my casual good looks, I've not had it easy. I grew up without a dad and my mum struggled to feed me and my brothers when we were kids. I've done a few jobs in my time. I've been a chippie, a stone mason, a holiday rep, you name it. Then I saw a job as a tutor in a prison and I took it on. Showing people how to build woodwork projects at the same time as rebuilding themselves was where I was meant to be. Working with lads like me who had started out with nothing and wanted to make something of themselves. I was lucky, though, because I had a family. And I wanted to say thank you to my mum who has held us all together . . .'

Unlike the majority of us, who are quietly leaking into our long fringes, his mum is openly sobbing in the audience. Bill leaps up out of his chair and stands beside him, gently slapping him on his back to stop the choking. A pause. Reverence. Then Thomas steps up to introduce me.

'As a topic, loss is a difficult one to think about. We are all affected by loss, in all its forms. We lose objects, fears, hopes, those we love. Yet out of loss comes strength. Losing everything leaves us a solid foundation upon which to build again. It shows us the value of what we have left as much as what we are missing. There are times when feelings of loss can overwhelm us and times when it can liberate. What is clear is that loss affects us all; to feel loss is to be human.

The impact of the competition has been surprising and as overwhelming as loss itself. From an idea based on sorrow to the resulting appearance of over a hundred entries in the categories of six-word stories, two hundred-word stories, art, and mixed media pieces. In being given just six words, ideas and thoughts on forms of loss could be held, contained, and expressed. The stories ranged from comic summaries of existing stories to poignant glimpses into other people's worst moments – something you will also see in the winner of the art category. We were honoured to read and see the entries, felt trusted with hidden stories, and also felt the weight of responsibility in choosing the images to feature with the stories.

We hope we have respected that trust in the exhibits you will soon see. For many reasons, there are no names on the exhibits. To own the stories is your choice, your own story to tell or not. The exhibition has become a story in its own right: one of community, a shared space of individual and common feelings. It has brought people together to form a visual connection between us.

Staff have also shared their own stories, showing that the legacy continues. What we hope is that the feelings and ideas found here will be acknowledged and supported. For support is here if you need it.'

Thomas has been standing behind me, ready to step in if I crack. His presence is welcome. It feels prickly to allow someone to stand behind me out of sightlines. No voices in my ear. Silent support. A rare feeling of being held without touch. The gift of being present in a place where no one really wants to be.

'So you may have noticed that you had to move a leaf-shaped Post-it note and a pen from your chair when you arrived. If you'd like to, you are welcome to write a note, a few words, or the name of someone or something you have lost. Then, as you leave the chapel to go to the exhibition, please put the note on the tree.'

I expected a rush to see who has won. But there is a respectful calm. No competitive canteen clamour. The men have lost their rush and the staff have lost their radio twitches. One by one we put a leaf on the tree. No names or identifiers. Just humans from the same roots, held together by the losses and gains that make us all. Drafts of movement breathe life into the mums, dads, grannies, dogs, homes branching out towards the light. Fears flutter with each new shoot of growth.

In the library, they find the stories slowly. Eased into the experience after careful planning, they are met with the gentler stories of losing fear before moving through the ones telling of lost loved ones, families, babies, homes, hope.

'I wish you had told me.'

'When will it stop hurting so?'

'I found light after the darkness.'

'You have to lose to win.'

'Gone from me far too soon.'

'The world is better without me.'

'She only took a few breaths.'

'I had to leave them behind.'

'My choices were not my own.'

'I did it all for them.'

'No one loves a sore loser.'

'When you lose, they all leave.'

'History always come back for more.'

'Losing it all to begin again.'

'My angels have killed my demons.'

We pour over the word-soaked salt memories held in a hundred and fifty wipe-clean laminated pockets. Including one from the deputy governor who didn't quite think it was possible. Wise elephant wrinkled eyes tell a different story. Over a quarter of the men gave in a form holding their emotions safely. Men of few words wrote longer pieces. Release before time served. Dean's enthusiasm poured into over twenty stories of lost hope and angels. Others summarised famous stories into six words and these appeared at the end of the exhibition.

' Mythical men fight dragons hoarding gold.'

'Finding lost worlds in wartime wardrobes.'

'The real monster was the doctor.'

'Every man has a dark side.'

'She lost her shoe at midnight.'

We ease tight shoes off and sit huddled in the library. Calm silence. Still no radios on. This has been a day of holding loss close, catching smoke hope before its coils are crushed by heavy air. These final tales raise the mood, holding the loss within a space safely. We haven't skirted around the realities of our condition. Frailty held up to the light and stared in the face. There has been a careful approach to the material. Distance when needed provided by guest judges who the men recognise and appreciate. They feel seen rather than watched. Acknowledged without being named. People not numbers. Community not anonymity.

We knew this was a rare moment. Even John took a seat to reflect. On how you could share deeply personal events without risking safety protocols. How you could walk the line between recognition and distance. It felt different going onto the wings to check in on a couple of men we'd noticed looking longingly at words worlds away. Dean was settled, sitting on his bed sketching. Ben was smiling quietly. He asked me for some paper to write to his lost mother and adrift son. Carl was playing pool, spinning colours from pockets like a child looking for sweets. Their entries were already stuck Marvel Milk style over bare breezeblock. Homespun glue sticking over the cracks for a while.

It was an exhibition of what happened when we remembered what we all were and what we could be. It became a place for translating the language of loss into the words of gain. My own writing mentor had come for the day. As a writer in residence at another private prison, he was keen to see what we'd done. How the other half lived. His surprise as Thomas stepped out from Prison Break and hugged me off my feet was a source of amusement for weeks afterwards. No harm done. It wouldn't happen in another prison. But for that day, things were different. There were no incidents. We'd lost tense alarm calls and pinched ears. We'd gained connections with no fear. Safely held in six words and the spaces between. What it means to lose and how we recover. Rebuild. Restore energy stocks. Take stock. Find what remains of the hoarded children.

I wondered how Dean felt about contributing so much yet not winning. But of course he was so much bigger than that.

That was a different day. I didn't mind that I didn't win. I'm bigger than that. It would take more than that to get me down. I am stronger than I was before. I won't give in again. I have turned my back on all that now. I won't be pulled away again. They won't pull me down. No matter how hard they try. It's all water off a duck's back now. I will rise like a phoenix from the ashes. Like I did before. I am burning to leave. I can see what I want to achieve. Not like them. Still caught in their games. Still tangled up in the scams, plots, trades, deals. I keep my distance now. Won't be drawn in. Just doing my own drawing. Making my own mark. Change the picture. Filling in the gaps with as much rainbow colour as I can. Because that's what I need. Bright stripes and lines of glitter. They block out the darkness.

10.

'Are you married, Miss?'

'Yes. But then you knew that already.'

'Happy?'

'Ecstatic.'

'If it changes . . .'

'Pretty sure it won't.'

'Just make sure.'

'Of what?'

Why did I ask? Caught off guard as I walk between wings, the sun peering round the edges.

'Just don't get caught with the bodies in the boot of your car. Get rid quickly. Don't hesitate.'

I pause. 'Not my style, Arthur.'

'I know, Mrs.'

We reach the door and he's still smiling. Grinning as he probably recalls in his head what a teacher told me later. You don't want to hang around with him. After what he did. He made his bed. He didn't let them lie in theirs.

He's not that person anymore. Double figures inside does that to a man. Prison pallor. Greyer than their sweatshirts, the lifers wore either bright workwear or their own clothes. A privilege earned over time. So much time. Long-serving officers were equally pale with shiny heads bobbing about with false humour. The same brave front. An equal chance of surviving beyond prison time. The average life span of a prison officer post-retirement is less than five years. No time at all.

No time to dwell on the grim statistics. No time to pause. Another lesson beckons. Time to get into character. Guard up. Earpiece in. Pinch myself. Same regime, different class. 'Stop me if you've heard this before'. With such a quick turnaround, it is difficult to remember what I have said to who. The rhythm of the lessons, planned to meet criteria and objectives, is automatic. Like driving home without remembering the journey. It leaves me free to focus on the men themselves. The different personalities that people the room. As you read this, you may wonder if these lessons were typical, standard days or specific moments. Actually, they are both. Teaching routine meets individuals. Performance targets colliding with the reality of trauma, abuse, violence, addiction, hope, and hate that bounced off the walls. Accommodating their needs and differences is a constant pressure and a welcome reward when they pass an exam, write a letter, smile, or even just show up.

Today's plan is a recap on letters, followed by idioms and language features. A familiar battle with words. I've become immersed in the shifting world of slang, meanings lurking in plain sight. Playing cards displayed in cell observation panels. 'King me', he says. A particular shopping list for the illicit pharmacy. If he's lucky, he'll get added powder and Persil. If not, cockroach powder. It is almost a shame that there are no functional skills lessons in chemistry. But then they would be redundant. The wings are full of chemistry professors, Walter Whites who can't spell but who can make a synthetic drug from cleaning products and whatever lays to hand. Handy fruit supplies became hooch, sped up by the fermenting accelerant brewed and sold in E Wing toilet bowls.

This group often reduces me to fits of laughter. Man's laughter is dangerous in a prison. Manslaughter just punctuation and a space away. Not so much for raised voices, which bring a flurry of officers' concern. More because I have had four children alongside the added pressure of a coffee-fuelled morning without a toilet break. And in a male prison, Tena Lady is in short supply. The last time I brought in my own was the last time I can remember laughing so hard I could have passed a mandatory drugs test or MDT. Piss easy. There we were, huddled over an Always panty liner (other brands are available) crying with soundless giggles at his feeble attempts to cut one up with children's plastic scissors. Neither of us could be arsed with getting the key to the cupboard for the key to the shadow board with the scissors and other sharps in. Let alone to then have to reverse the process. Twice. It seemed totally normal to be asked if I could give one to a colleague as he had forgotten his pant liners. I learnt that his armpits were hiding a secret.

Sweat-soaked in a fairy hammock each day. And with that day being a scorcher, he was in perspiration street by noon.

'*Assistance required. Education office. Teacher down.*'

Unable to breath for crying. Code Blue with swear words. Fuck me. That was not what I expected to be doing in a Cat C prison on this Thursday afternoon. Perhaps a Monday. Anything went on Mondays. The day of simmering tensions from the weekend, poised for family visits the next day.

Humour has become a survival mechanism. A way of releasing tension when all else is held back. Held in suspended disbelief. Sitting at the back of the class, waiting. Slowly, it puts its hand up. Do you know what they have done? How many ways there are to kill a man? Death by dangerous. Car. Bullet. Knife. The ways to kill a woman were more diverse. Stones. Poison. Overdose. Fists. Pillow fights smothering with love. I can't even speak of the others. Smaller, younger voices, some barely able to form words. The image of them leaves me speechless. Makes me hug mine just that little bit tighter at bedtime. I try to block them out, too. But they sneak in through stories, reminders of another life.

'Miss?'

'I told you, it's Kate. Dr Kate if you piss me off.'

'Miss Kate?'

'Yes.'

'Do you teach your own kids, like?'

'God no!'

'Makes sense. Poor sods.'

'Thanks. Now back to idioms.'

'Did you just call me an idiot?' Wry grin.

'Nope. I'll keep that line in my back pocket for later.'

'Miss, you ain't got pockets.'

'And that's an idiom.'

Now they are sighing.

We rattle through English, Polish, Scottish, and Cuban idioms. My new one for the day is Bulgarian.

'It's break time.'

'Tell us something we don't know. Something we haven't hoped for. Captain Obvious has discovered America!'

I scuttle back to the staff room for a quick coffee, which I regret as soon as I get back in the classroom. Legs crossed for a further three hours. Fingers already crossed we can get to the outcomes in time for release back to the wings.

'Miss. Idioms are . . .'

'Remember the agreement. No swearing. Keep it PG.' I could murder a tea.

'Crap, Miss.'

'Dead obvious.'

'What if you have autism?'

Bit awkward. Like the time I said I had dropped a bollock at work and the shock in my friend's eyes was hard to explain. You mean you have them? And they are detachable? Did you find it again? Is it lost forever? 'But what if English isn't your first language? How do you know what they mean?'

'Like?'

'It so happens that I have some on cards I made earlier.'

'Of course you fuckin' have.'

'Let's go through them.'

'The elephant in the room.'

'We ain't talking about that.'

'Nicely explained.'

But Uri looks puzzled.

'What does mean? Where is elephant? Is Miss? She not look fat?'

And that is when I lose control of the class. Laughter. Proper belly laughs and wheezing squeals leak out everywhere. I cling to the edge of my desk, silently laughing and praying that my Tena Lady holds out. Wrinkles from laughter lines have become ingrained in my elephant hide. So perhaps Uri was right.

I held a whole herd of elephants marching around as hunters pick them off one by one. And I was bone tired of juggling elephants. Each one had a name. Class, trauma, privilege, gender. By far the heaviest was race. Despite all our human connections, I was still white. Standing, grey-haired and wrinkled, carrying keys and, with them, all the power. I could reduce their privileges back to basic, put them on a charge incurring extra days, influence probation decisions, argue for hostel places. I wouldn't do any of these things lightly, if ever. Acutely aware of how endemic racism has shaped the trauma journeys of the men from Black British families, I was in a suspended position of privilege. But I didn't enjoy the position, unlike a few of the over-zealous officers keen to impress their power. Putting people in their place, eyeball to eyeball at bang-up, jingling keys loudly along the landings.

There, I felt at home. The feeling of being secondary. Vulnerable, but in recognisable surroundings. The same dreary yellow walls of my 1970s childhood. Of being locked in a room. Of being controlled by others. Being kept inside under the guise of safety. An overbearing female presence. It hadn't escaped my notice that I was working in Her Majesty's Prison. A female space, which held men childlike. Curled up and foetal in cells. Screaming to be heard and fed and changed. Powerless but shaping their surroundings. Scribbled walls and far-flung shit. On a good day. Of which there were many.

On the other days, the boundaries slipped to show the chinks in our armour. They say you need cracks in the dark to let the light in. In prison, things were upside down. Dean's glimpses of darkness crept in disguised as the light. What the numbness blocked was the connection to others. They recognised the fractures papered over with pages of words. Dean knew more than I realised.

She's falling faster and I'm going soon. Won't be able to catch her soon. I'm out but I'm not down. I've got a plan, dreams, plots, desires I need to get on with. I try to be friends with everyone and spread some positivity in the dark. I try not to let the darkness

win. Don't get me wrong. I could go back and it would be fun.
But I won't. I've got a plan to paint the outside all the colours I
can't get here. Red, green, blue, pink, yellow. Black for the edges
to hold it all in. Keep it close. Don't let it go over the lines. Not like
the picture I'm working on. Words. All different, opposites, same,
colours, wavy, straight, dark, light. Like the inside of my head, it
spins and I find the order of things. Put them down and nail them
to a board and move on.

Today I see a wolf in puppy fur. Kind eyes surrounded by wild
white hair. A grey Santa Claus bringing cheer to my classroom.
Samuel leans against the rails. His hands are clasped as if in
prayer over the edge. Today he seems distracted. No offers to
help others or hand things out. The light in his eyes has faded
to a small pin prick. Dark tunnel vision. But is it a light or an
oncoming train?

'I need to go to the chapel.'

'After the lesson?'

'At three. That's when it needs to be.'

I can see his lips narrow under his beard. I have to ask why.

'I need to light a candle.'

I don't answer. I know by now what that means. Here comes
the train. Loaded with loss, baggage, and dead letters without
destination. I picture it as a steam train, puffing and sighing
up a hill, pistons powering it ever onward. No children waving
by the trackside. No time to stop. It never stops. Ploughing

through the lost families, throwing them all up in the air, suspended until time. Pressure cooker filled with cheap hock joints trying to eke out the week. Held in. Lack and loaded feelings of what has happened between. Trapped air build up until a release. Weight levered off with a fork. Keep a lid on it while the plumes breathe outward. Souls set free while the flesh and bone lies at the bottom of a metal furnace. All the passion, fire and feelings held in a tin can tomb. Once regret pierced, they begin to fester.

'It's for him.'

I still don't speak. Just smile in acknowledgement. Father? Son? Brother? Lover? The train keeps going.

'Been eight years to the day. To the time. Since the murder.'

Then there is a judder. Points failure. Eyebrows raise. This one is different. It's a memorial for a relative stranger and the moment of their death. The act which brought him inside from the cold.

Standing next to me is the gentlest murderer I have met so far. Here are remorse and regret bound in skin, hair, and bone. Not spilling his guts out like the others had for sympathy. Held together. Introspective.

I'm still inside myself as the plastic tray hits the table and Lynne flumps into the chair next to me.

'Whatever are you thinking about?'

'Just work stuff.'

'You look way too pale for that top. Fancy a coffee?'

'Can do.'

'So my day has been rubbish. Total wash out. I am so sick of getting nowhere with work.'

'Two steps forward?'

'Oh absolutely. Why can't people just be honest?'

'Because it's never that simple.'

'Why not, though?'

'Because we believe our own stories. I was writing a short story with someone today. It was a tragic tale of how he lost his wife and children in an accident. He even added a dead dog into the equation.'

'Was it about him?'

'Of course. We put it all on paper and closed the book until next time. If I can stomach it.'

'I mean who wouldn't be moved by that. But to lose everyone. And then your dog . . .'

'That's what did it.'

'I can imagine.'

'It's not that simple.'

'Why ever not? I can't believe you of all people would say that. I mean. You've changed but not that much, darling. I'm the callous one. Didn't you get the memo? Maybe you could introduce us? You know I love a man in uniform.'

'It wasn't a colleague. Staff, I mean.'

'Oh my God! Why didn't you tell me that in the first place? If I'd have known that I would never have—'

'I shouldn't have said anything. I'm just tired. Too tired to hold it back.'

'Hold back what?'

'It doesn't matter.'

'It does now. You can't leave me hanging. I want to know the ending. Does he get his just desserts? Actually, speaking of desserts, do you fancy a cake? I'm going to grab a slice of that cheesecake. Sod the diet. Do you want one?'

She's already in the queue. Distant.

'Look at what you've made me do. It'll take an hour on that treadmill to work this off! Are you sure you don't want anything? You're wasting away you lucky cow!'

'I wish.'

'So anyway, you were going to tell me the ending, weren't you? I'm not going to let you get away with it. Not this time.'

'It isn't a happy one.'

'None of your stories are, you know. You need to be more positive. Count your blessings. I mean there are plenty worse off than you. It's that place. It's no good for you.'

'It's not all bad. Just some days.'

'So . . .'

'I'm too tired to argue.' The adrenaline slump has hit. Blood sugar is low.

'So don't. You know I always win in the end.'

'Unlike my storyteller, then.'

'Oh, for the love of God and the Kardashians, spit it out!'

'Most of it was true. His story. He just forgot the bit where he was driving them into a post. On purpose.'

'You're kidding!'

'I wish I was, Lynne.' No, really. I wish I was her sometimes. Simple black and white stories. Not knowing the in-between.

'So was that why he was inside? Of course it was. Lying swine. They are all the same. All mouth and no trousers. That poor woman. I know the type. I bet she walked into a few doors. And those poor children. Hearing it all. What else was he hiding?'

'I didn't . . . realise.' Then the penny drops, elephant's jawbone falls to the floor. Here she is. A ghosted survivor of more than voices.

'Oh it's all in the past now. I wouldn't waste any time thinking about him. Wouldn't give him the satisfaction. I hope he rots. He's in Hell now. He bloody should be.'

'So you never . . . no one reported him?'

'Never said a word. I wonder if she knew we heard it all.'

'I'm sorry.'

'Oh don't be. I'm not. Come along. No use moping about when we could be out and about. We've been here too long.'

My life so far is reduced to a three-page CV. Name, address, phone numbers, email, and then on to all the places I have been. All the spaces between. Carers leave. Ghosted mother. Haunted child. Maternity hat trick plus extra time into penalties. Referees. Only it shouldn't be here. I'm looking at my

time with fear. It's here plain as my need to pee. Urgent. Panic.
John looks back at me and says it will be fine. No one will have
seen it on the top of a pile of papers in the storeroom.

But I know how many people have been in there. It's right
opposite my classroom. Trusted prisoners boxing up old
records not their own. A civilian worker and a young officer.
Smiling more as they left, misbuttoned blouse, and belt a notch
tighter. I storm shaken into the office. There are apologies.
Much shredding of nerves and papers.

I'm trying to stay calm. To forget the security breach.
Because it isn't just about my security. It's about my family. My
kids. My former colleagues now friends. All the people I try
to lock out. Ignore. Ghosted from this other life. They flicker
into view when a learner mentions a place, their home, missing
school sports day, parents' evening. I can't speak, squeaking the
door open to usher in the next wave.

Holding the door open, I can see a figure coming towards
me. I taught him a few months ago and he was a model pupil.
Mine dilated on learning how he appeared in others' eyes. He
was responsible for running the streets my feet know by name.
He's already been in this morning and we've been reminded
to keep him out by security. Two breaches in one day aren't an
option. I put my foot against the door and hold it open a little
way. Luckily, this is one door which opens inward.

'Sorry Andy, you know you can't come in today.'

'Miss. I need to go to the library.'

'Another day. When it's your wing's turn maybe. Not today.'

His pad mate and crew stand back a little way. His eyes narrow.

'Let me in.'

'You know I can't. Sorry.'

'You will be.'

Pause.

'I know where you live.'

I push the door closed and he makes a sign. Fingers round a gun.

Warning taken, I leave without one. Two weeks' holiday owing are brought forward. Fast spinning cells while I am gone. The words were enough. They always are. I write my way out of the chaos with scrambled dead letters and living eulogies. All our phones are red flagged by the police. No words needed if we dial for help. Silent night screams. Sweat tides marked sheets of paper written in insomnia. No rest for the broken.

When I go back, tiptoeing clunky boots, I'm greeted by the same figure at the door. Hand on heart and radio, we decide to step into the breach we have made for ourselves.

I move outside, sliding past the rare sight of an officer on the door with a list of the roll allowed into Education.

'Morning, Andy. How are you?'

'I think we need to clear the air, Miss.'

'I'd like that, Andy.'

'You dissed me in front of my friends. That wasn't on.'

'I'm sorry I couldn't let you in. I know your friends thought it was off. But I didn't. Are we OK now?'

'We are.'

'I'm glad.' Wait for the trade-off. It doesn't come.

'The others missed you, Miss. So, we good.'

'Well, we're both working on that. How've you been?'

'Leaving next week.'

'Gate nerves?'

'Bit. Wondering what I be doing next.'

'Something different, I hope. Weren't you into music? I heard you were pretty good. And now you have more stories to tell. I'm not going to say it's a badge of honour, but you know what I mean. Do your music properly. Let it take you away from the other things that brought you here. You know?'

'Do you think I could?'

'Why not? Always worth a shot.'

He grins.

'Not that kind of shot. I am looking forward to seeing you on a different scene.'

'It could work, Miss. Safe. We'll see.'

The next time I see his face is in an online magazine. He's a fully-fledged musician. But he is on the out and doing well. My happiness for him is short-lived. You'd think this is our happy ending but the damage is already done. Because while I was away, Dean was released without goodbyes. A double ghosting. I look at the painting he left me of words in different fonts. Inscribed 'To my friend Kate – don't ever change' the words spin and fix in various moods. Sometimes I notice 'academic', 'angel', 'legend', 'serenity'. Other days I find 'aggy', 'criminal', 'fate', 'stupid', 'upside down', 'silent'.

11.

Get up. Eyes wide open. Light up the dark. Crackling bones and slow heartbeat. Grating knees. Defrost. Thaw thoughts of what might lie ahead. Driving in the wrong direction to collect my work husband John. Dragonbreath day dissolves into winter morning, warning of more snow. If we can get to the roundabout, then we are taken in by Land Rovers. It's not as if the students can't get in. Always there. No terms. No holidays. No time off for good behaviour for teachers. Ready for mischief. Ready to teach me. And a warm classroom means even more on days running close to Christmas. Melting tears on razor wire as we arrive.

You shouldn't begin with the weather. It makes for a poor, stilted conversation and a bad book. But here, the weather frames the day's possibilities. If it begins to snow, we watch the windows. Earpieces pressed for a call to finish. Get home. Find the way back through winding slush roads. Follow the yellow road round. It's not about the journey. It's the destination. There's no place like home. My empathy with my fellow students doesn't quite stretch to staying overnight. Any stony port in a storm. It should make the ideal writing retreat. No distractions. Four walls of blank white slate. Pure driven snow mud smudged outside bleeds in through the gates. Familiar mustard doors and blue walls greet me with peering eyelids. Here I am welcomed with bleary grins. There are no piles of boxes hemming me in. No talk of clearing up memories into a skip. Here we hold on. Nothing gets left behind. That's already happened. Rebuilding, not dismantling. Piece by piece the puzzles of my childhood home are reforming. Cracks from weighty contents close up. Holes from bolts filled in. Inside, I can begin again. Each shift hallmarked, date-stamped, and sourced. Registered for quality. The patina is polished to glory or left to tarnish in polluting air. Same object, different setting. Routine chaos. No Dean.

Leave the phone behind. Pull on my belt. Adjust the radio and key holder. Check the chain and whistle. Wolf whistle as I bend down to pick up the fallen inhaler. Today I'm struggling for air. Blame it on the cold. Numb head, thawing heart as we leave the airlock doors behind. Pick up my keys. Radio on. Leave behind my name. Tally up the cost so far this month. Belt needs another hole. Boring meetings. Ringing ear now sings all night. Pinch myself. Ear clutches the single headphone. One-sided versions of what is happening around me. Biased, twisted words cable through clothes to clip into my hip. Half-stories. Half life. Half-death left behind at the house.

I'm stretched between three houses. The sleep of home,

prison life, and childhood death. The holding of photos. The pasts we take forward. What we leave behind. Packed boxes waiting. Stuffed under the bed. Paper monsters. All life held in ink. Stories of selves unknown and pieced together. I'd managed to keep them all separate until that call. Then the worlds collided. The walls broke between inside and outside. I saw why I loved the prison work. And why it was slowly killing me. Skin folded envelopes sealing in a tiredness that would not leave my bones, no matter how much sleep I had. My lifeblood was found in clear bags of words, books, and gym kit. Evidence bags hanging on hooks for later. Feeding my spirit. Ghosted each day to return again. No chance to settle. Always alert. Always holding on to something. Radio. Keys. Pen. Hope. Books. Pee. Tongue. Never a person. Always at arm's length. Tattooed ink friends, permanent yet skin deep.

Lesson 6 of 25 (Ideally) New form, same dynamics.

Learners: 9.

Differentiation: 3xADHD, 1xASD, 2xDyslexic, 10xSEMH.

Topic: Types of Text.

Aims: To identify four main types of text: Informative, Descriptive, Persuasive, Instructive.

Outcomes: Complete a discussion on advertising. Work in groups. Not to leave the classroom as you found it. Be more savvy. Reflect more. Notice more. Speak more. Connect more.

'What's with all the adverts?'

'Can we make a pizza from the recipe?'

'This one is obvious. It's information. See? Numbers. Fifty percent of people like this chocolate.'

'So what about the other fifty percent?'

'Ah. Well maybe they love it? Hate it? Never had it?'

'Is this how you use our feedback forms to keep your job, Miss?'

'Absolutely. If only fifty-one percent of you said you gained something, then I would say "over half" were satisfied.'

'That's cheating, Miss.'

'No. That's persuasive writing. Once you've cracked the code, you become smarter at spotting bullshit.'

'What else is there?'

'Look at the papers here. Which one would you buy?'

'The one with big writing. That says it's 25p . . . Oh, cheaper than the others. That's sly. Man didn't notice.'

'Why not?'

'Font. Smaller. I need glasses.'

'Shall we fill in an app to get some? Have you had them before?'

'Yeah. Still in my prop box.'

So near but so far. Still in a marked box at reception, two walls away. The foot-moulded shoes holding his journey interrupted. Clothes and wallet. Traces of life left.

'Let's get them, then.'

'We'll see.'

We shall. The world of grey mist will have edges. Smeared floors will shape into crumb-filled piles. Chicken bones and blue plastic plates. Abandoned picnics. Tables wiped clean for the next day.

'*Release for Education break.*'

I've learnt enough today already. About the ways we hide weakness. The ways we avoid disclosure. Finding ways around rather than through. Of prop boxes and memory boxes. Ill-fitting court suits which hang off chewed old bones on release. Fresh-faced recognition of ID gone sour.

There's a new, young officer on the landing and we exchange names as my men scatter out of the door. All but one. He walks up to the railings. His stride has a purpose. We all exchange glances. He puts his foot on the bottom rung, swinging his body, child on a bridge to look over at the drowning sea.

'Are you OK, Pete?'

'No.'

'Can you come over here and talk?'

'No.'

'Can I stand here then?'

'Yes. I suppose. It's a free country.'

Not in here though. Hand moves over my radio. Underhand but seen by the officer, who stays back, ready. He knows what I am thinking. Because he is thinking the same.

'Pete. What's up?'

'I feel like I did before.'

Before when? Before being inside? Before I knew him?

Before he knew what he had done? Before he knew he would leave prison homeless?

'How so? Tell me. I'm here.'

'When I had the pills and took 'em all.'

'Have you got any now? Back in your pad?'

'I have some. Not enough cheeked so far. Soon though. Unless . . .'

'Tell me about it. Over here where it's quieter.'

I can see a few side-eyes nodding in our direction.

'What if I don't want to?'

'You'll make me proper mardy for the rest of the day.'

'It's OK, Kate. You'll get over it.'

In one move, he is up. Pivoting over the rail. He's nearly over as I grab him. Pull him back. Top then shoulders grabbed from behind. We stagger backwards. I don't let go. I wonder if he still thinks about it. Moving backwards was in the training. To keep me safe. Other way round now. He is safe. I realise I am not OK. Life and death in one moment. No boundaries. Me in between.

We talk in hushed voices as the other men carry on chatting. Show's over. Same performance with a matinee on Saturday on the wing. What we have got used to scares me. Dread trickling into my toes. Keeps me grounded in a place of flying men. We talk of what happened. What he wants to happen next. What has to happen. The officer walks carefully closer. He has been hovering, keeping watch on the others. I ask him to stay with Pete. Straighten my cardigan and skirt. And walk calmly to the unit. Unlock the door. Lock the door again behind me. Walk into my manager's office.

'Fuck.'

'Great opener, Kate. Any more?'

'Plenty. Shit. Balls. Willies. Twazzock. Cockwombles.'

'Not the best lesson so far then?'

'Your powers of perception are in excellent form. I need you to make a call. Get the Safer Custody team here. Now. Please.'

His turn. 'Fuck.'

I explain what happened. The bare facts. No flowery idioms, similes, or metaphors. I'd fail my own functional skills exam. Cross-examination later is fine. It's on the hoof and wing, not in a coroner's court.

Straighten my hair. Untangle my radio and unlock the door. Walk through it. In the character of a calm teacher. Lock the door. Push down the realisation. Pete is standing with the officer. He is handed over to the mental health team who have arrived. A rare break for them has been filled with another story. Better ending this time. I thank the officer for being around and for his quiet calm in keeping the others away. Lucky. Normally we are on our own. Left to remember Suicide and Self-Harm Training 101 in all its red glory. Don't leave them on their own. Remember all that is said and done. Just the facts to put on record. No extras. No assumptions. No 'I think'. Which is easy now. Because I don't think. It's all instinct. Alert eyes. Twitching ears. Action.

'Have they called movement yet, Miss?'

'Are you kidding? We've got another fun-filled forty minutes of idioms left to go.'

'Are you taking the piss?'

'You been to the toilet before we go back in?'

'Dropped the kids off at the pool, Miss.'

'There's one. Off we go.'

Masks on. Silent witnesses to the events of breaktime. That will teach me to hope for a pee break. Maybe even coffee. We battle through spelling and progress reports.

'We doing OK, Miss?'

'Aren't we?'

I'm not sure I am. Well, we're still here. In a shabby classroom, bedraggled plants hanging from the edges. Dusty floor. Short stories around the room.

'We've got five minutes left, Miss.'

'Can we go early?'

'Nope. No one is leaving yet. Creative writing time.'

Mock groans and real despair.

'If today was a colour, what would it be? Describe it like a posh paint colour.'

'Like that poncey Farrow and Ball stuff? Used to be a painter, Miss.'

'You still are. Just the medium has changed.'

'Nah, Miss. I'm large.'

'Fabulous. And let's keep that one under wraps, eh?'

'OK, Miss.'

'Snot Green.'

'Newborn Nappy Yellow.'

'Sea Pier Brown.'

'On Road Grey.'

'Dragon Heart Black.'

'Slipstream Blue.'

'Escape Rope Fawn.'

'*Release from Labour and Education.*'

Tumbling out to greet the frosting walkways. Pale faces shrink a little.

One looks back.

'What's your colour for today, Miss?'

Blood Brain Spatter. Bleep. Slime Slip Green. Bleep. Coal Dust Grey. Bleep. Mine Black. Lost Blue Sea. Bleep. Lifejacket Orange. Bleep. Un-brilliant White. Radio Black. Dead Battery Brown.

'Eggshell Blue. Thanks for asking, Cal. Have a safe evening. See you next lesson.'

'Like what you did there. Not see you on Monday. Because you never know.'

Grey merges into the oncoming fog. It's time to go home before the storm hits.

We are snowbound for the next three days. Wrapped in jumpers at home. A chance to reflect. No easy sleep. Handing Pete to the prison team helped me leave. Put the awkward spin searches he will have for pills to the back of my already churned mind. I checked in on him later the same day and he was out on the landings drinking coffee. He nodded. Turned to his neighbour and I walked away. Orange folder in the office. Verbal and written reports submitted. I could walk away easier. Welly boot trudge to return later. Home was crammed with boxes brought back from Dad's to sort through. Sifting sands of time. Mouse nests and snake pits in steel trunks. Banging lids shut. Different bruises. No one knows what to say. So we stay quiet. Wordless. Worldless. In between life and death until the funeral has passed. Away. Gone in a wing beat. Fluttering dragonfly between tables of different groups: church, Lions, and mice. Nibbling sandwiches as sausage roll skin flakes fall onto hard ground. I'm on autopilot outside. Paperwork, clearing, signing, drowning. Dusty dreams. Boxes of cartridges, pen, and gun. Gas canisters that might come in handy. Heavy upright piano. Upstanding citizens support. Firewood family furniture. Wearing a mask of grief. A face-covering shroud.

'It's very difficult to know where to begin – to start with a boy who was expelled from nursery for being a disruptive influence, or to end with a seventy-nine year-old who never retired. Perhaps I should start as he did on our wedding speech by saying, "Now I know how Daniel felt going into the lion's den". He was not too fond of public speaking or indeed of being in the limelight, yet he was president of Lions seven times. My dad was a complex man: a proud Brexiteer whose last job was funded by the EU. Of course, it was the love of tinkering and adapting hospital tools, beds, and toys for differently abled children that sparked his interest. He was peaceful yet loved firearms. A devout Christian who toyed with the idea of a Viking burial on a burning ship. So today could have been very different. He had a penchant for nurturing plants and birds, but also a taste for blowing things up. His joy at showing his granddaughter how to explode a bottle of cola by dropping a mint in it was a fun moment – and one which filled us full of dread as she casually asked for Polos on the return journey halfway down the M6 motorway. His library of books covered subjects as diverse as the classics to his favourite poems, *Old Possum's Book of Practical Cats*. He was loving but fond of provoking comments. He left so many stories untold yet loved to tell the same ones again and again – the story of how my mum held up the local police station by handing in his beloved rifles is one that I'm sure many have heard. He was proud of his dad avoiding the carnage at Dunkirk by commandeering a lorry and driving eleven men to a different harbour to get back home two days before a black-edged telegraph arrived announcing him missing presumed dead. Dad's own driving abilities were somewhat frustrated by mine and my brother's travel sickness, limiting his radius to about thirteen miles in an old Morris Minor. Not daunted, Mum and Dad bought a caravan and found a site next to the river Dane where we had several family holidays, saw kingfishers, and heard my dad use his best Anglo-Saxon when my brother kicked his football into the river. Twice.'

That eulogy is over and out. Pasted into a scrapbook

of official lines. True but not all of it. There are other things surfacing. Waves wash over and pull out to sea leaving gritty toes. There are things he didn't teach me before he left. Like how to cook vinegar-soaked conkers to win any fight. How to bake a cake rather than a brown-ringer. How to identify all the stars in the sky, not just the major and minor bears. How to name all the cloud types whilst watching them all drift by or loom overheard. How to name all the wildflowers winding round germander speedwell and flax. I need to know how to listen to all the words, to find the stories snatched and glimpsed between the door cracks. How to knit one, pearl one now – I'm ready to be patient. How to sew straight, go over the lines, and tailor the edges to suit. To make jam that sets like the sun sleeping in jars. How to make do and mend, stay still, and sit with myself amidst the bustle of days dreamt. How to open the box. Clear up, clear out, and clear off. Close the door and go on.

My outside self is locked away. I've posted the keys back through the newly replaced front door and said goodbye. Inside, storied thoughts stack up in high-rises. The lifts aren't working. Each step upwards a breathless grunt, knee click away from the ground. And inside prison, I feel the stones in between my toes. Sneaking into flowered boots, they jab at my soul.

The numbness shrouds words muffled into underwater backdrops. The voices that can't pierce the elephant skin made real by habit. Nothing from the outside gets in. Light can't find any cracks. Dean's words sit in a prop box in between the gate and the sunlight. Packed in a plastic bag, labelled for later:

'Kate. You're awesome and my friend for life. Facto!! Thanks for all your support and inspiring encouragement. There are still things you haven't taught me. I can stay away from the darkness but I don't know how long for. How do I find the others who share my passions, loves, art, pictures, words? How do I keep burning bright until I can start art school? How do I stay up all night to paint without racking up my mum's bills? How do I stay quiet? How do I deal with the quiet? It's so quiet and no one wants to talk. They're all jealous of where I want to be. How do I not let them in? How do I learn to wait? To sit still and let the thoughts build up. They are coming for me. The false friends and people from before. From that other life which keeps trying to tempt me back again. The demons are coming back from inside. I am still twice born.'

Sitting in a memorial for another lost man, I curl my feet around the caught shoe pebbles waiting for the end of the ceremony. One by one, men speak of his support for others. His generosity and courage. At the front, his family sit. Awash with emotions. They have had no funeral yet. Watching a feather spin caught on a skylight cobweb, his presence is still felt. Here I cry and stay to sit with the men left to pray before trailing off. Alone in cells next to where he was found, mourning a morning loss, they sit, heads bowed. We light candles. Side-by-side with Mal, who also lost his father in the last few shivering weeks. My freezeframe tattoo catches his eye.

'It's funny, Miss.'

'What is?'

'The best memory I have of him is fishing. Before he left for good. We sat for hours in silence. A dragonfly landed between us. He said if I saw another, I should remember him. And here you are. Watching over me. A dragonfly.'

No words. None needed.

Words settled later in each passing day. Passing his hunched body over the mop and bucket. He cleaned the wing I visited regularly. He didn't know when he was leaving. Another IPP prisoner caught in time. Stuck. Stretched out wings ready to fly. His smile weakened each week. Colours fading in glass-fractured outlines. Of course, I left before he did.

Sitting in a Saturday café, I people-watch through the glass. All on their phones or laptops. Just one couple talking about new gazebos and the stress of not having the pool cleaned this month. The lines furrowed just as deep as the men wrestling demons and angels. No such thing as perspective. And who am I to judge? I hide my issues in dusty tissue paper boxes. Underneath photos of proud ancestors on scrubbed doorsteps. The same old house slowly crumbling into the mine shafts under it. Undermined by meagre seamstress' subsistence. Unpaid invoices for sequin dresses she could never afford herself. A woman buried under the bodies of others' costumed lives. Amongst my dad's things, I find pocketbooks of measurements, lists of material and findings needed. All that lay between these women was a sheer silk fabric, long line dress. Keeping both in clothes. My grandma's house had an outside toilet, soot trails, blanket at the window, no electricity. Welcoming damp brick smell and watery floors. There it is. The familiarity of work. The odour of what is left when all the trappings of wealth and status have been taken away. Except she never had them to begin with. It didn't matter. We'd work with what we had to make what we needed. Elastic band footballs, paper decorations, makeshift cards. All in a day's work for a prisoner too.

Even out of work, my head is there. Sustain the alert-mode until the weekend. Two blissful nights without ear-clipped alarms to follow in a few hours of sleep. Light-headed, heavy-footed, twisted in the middle. A body stretched to the limits. In my head I'm bridging the houses of sleep, childhood, and correction. Actually, no. Wait. That can't be right. It shouldn't be. But ever since that call, the walls have broken down. The door shattered. The fence fallen in. No boundaries. I was turning inside out. Raw emotions have appeared on the wing, flying through starling murmuration in writing sessions. Connections in synchronised pens. Scribbling of poems present, raps, and gaps in knowing. Sometimes there are no words. Iridescent colours all the same. None different for that short hour at a time. Soaring over charred buildings and fields of pollen-laden yellow. Until it was time to pack up. Pulling the radio puppet strings out. Turning sleeves back from outside in. Going outside to see the rooks gathering in lines on the roof tiles. Return dead radio. Recharge.

This little spot of me-time rings and whirs in my ear. I still sit with my back to the wall, door in view. I've turned to check the front door twice already this morning, delaying leaving. Proving I'm closed off. The absence of my work belt weighs heavy. Missing that reminder of feeling safe, surrounded by friends. Problems not my own. Ones I can support or hand over. Nothing left unfinished at the end of each day. Unless it's the weekend. Routines gone. Left undirected. Jumping when I hear a fire alarm. Seeing smokers breathing forbidden luxuries in my face as I walk past. Objects to buy, look at, touch, buy, buy more. And some spare for later. Just in case. Buy one, get two free. Boxes and boxes of toilet rolls and salmon. Prepare for the apocalypse. A crapalanche of stuff is falling from my eyes. Even in the café, I spot bags of clothes and accessories. How many clutch bags can you need? Clutching at life's meaning through material things. Things to hold on to. Keep close. When all else is lost.

I clutch an empty coffee cup. No Lynne today. I struggle to be around her. I don't know what to say. And neither does she. Her storied silence disrupts my inside world of empathy. I don't have the emotional bandwidth to wrestle with the silent ones. The survivors. I've ghosted them and I'm not proud of that. I've recognised their safety needs and not been coerced into giving out addresses. I know they exist behind the screen's words, index crimes filed away and spilling over as quickly as I emptied the boxes from home. But I haven't listened. I can't. It is too much.

Should I have another coffee and watch the world's stillness as I spin round? A phone buzzes. Contraband! Shit, it's me. Grimace. Scan the room. No one has even noticed. It's Liz. She shouldn't have one either! Swipe the shaking screen.

'Hello?'

'Kate. Are you alone?'

'Eeer, yes. You aren't going to start heavy breathing, are you?'

'Kate. I . . .'

'Are you OK?'

'Have you . . . heard?'

'About what?'

'I wanted to tell you. I didn't want you to hear it...'

'Hear what? Are we to get yet another top boss? New paperwork? It never stops does it.'

'It's Dean.'

Radio silence.

'He's dead. Dead, Kate.'

'But . . .'

'He took his own life this morning. His mum found him.'

'Are you sure?'

Of course she is. She's wobbling on the end of the line. All I can see are rainbows and paintings and glitter and graffiti and words. Laughter so loud you could see it coming. Not him. Not the happy one. The one who scooped others up in a sweat-glistened hug. Held me in his wide eyes when that other call came through.

'I can't believe it either.'

'Are you OK?'

'No. We are not OK.'

'What do we do? What can we do?'

We both trail off.

Sit down. Take a breath. Then another. Maybe one more before stopping. Numb. I can't feel. I stupidly try to get up. On the floor I crouch down. Maybe if I prayed it wouldn't be true. That I'm in that dream state of waking sleep again. Now people are looking. Scoop myself back into the fake leather chair. Lean into the arm. It's all false. Tidal chatter wave washes over. Eyes closing. Moments slip by. I pull myself up by the coat sleeves, inside out again. Spilling over the sides. Bursting at the seams.

He's gone. Left us. Twice. How could that happen? How could he go from the promise of art school to a blank page? Away from the dangers of prison. He was the enthusiastic one. The loud one. Not the quiet one with an orange folder. Trails of blue vapour and yellow stars falling behind him as he walked. How did he dissolve? Why? I'm cell-spun confused with the knowing what I have always feared.

I stare at my phone. Focus on the dancing apps for comfort. Split up. Look for clues. He was there. Lying in the Messenger dump for spam, nudes, and unsolicited requests. The phone I never use anymore because I've been conditioned to think I shouldn't have it. Hidden from sight. His last words:

'Hey my amazing kate its'

'pretty awesome out here'

'isn't it'

'Loves ya x'

A string of joy unbounded by grammar or apostrophes. Unanswered. Uncorrected. Undeleted.

12.

'It's OK for you. Just carry on walking.'

I know that voice. It doesn't belong on a cold Saturday street. Breath coiling upwards as I look up and across the cobbled lump kerb.

'Spare some change? For me and my pregnant girlfriend?'

We could walk past, carried by the wave of Christmas shoppers keen to get home. Annie is certainly being dragged down by way too many bags from what is our annual trawl around the shops. I won't see her again for months as she vanishes under the weight of family calendars. Our separation is as much my fault as hers. I've been inside for so long that it's easier to stay there than manage the come-down and work up each weekend. My Christmas cards are full of 'must get together soon' whilst I am falling apart at saggy seams.

The market is closing and the homeless are pushing against the tide to return to their usual haunts. They have been moved on, out of sight from tourists during the day. I can see Simon, the veteran who has taken up his familiar post by the façade of

Debenhams. I've already got him a coffee, milk and two sugars as he likes it.

But this voice is one I know from another time and place. I peer through the woolly inspection panel of my scarf and bobble hat. Walking towards the pile of sleeping bags, I can make out a gaunt man with a woman fallen curled up on his lap. Familiar eyes meet.

'Hello, George.'

'Do you recognise me?'

'Of course I do. You were my peer mentor for four months. My colleague. How are you here?'

'We lost our hostel place. This is Kay. She's thirty-five weeks' pregnant.'

The bundle of bags rustles a little. She is still asleep.

How is this happening?

For not the first time in seeing George, I am lost for words. But here he is. His normal kindness and warmth leaving his body fast. It's already minus four degrees.

I don't know what to say or do. I look at the lesions on his face and ask him, faded to jaded eye, 'Are you using again? Or dealing?'

'No. Or we aren't allowed in the shelter tonight.' His clear eyes sinking into skin tell me he is still honest.

'How much is it?'

'It's thirty-eight pounds for both of us. We have to sleep apart and we hate that. We feel safer together. But it's too cold to stay outside.'

'Christ. Where do you normally sleep? I don't mean to be nosey but . . .'

He smiles. 'I know. You're the first person who has spoken to me today. We normally sleep behind Sofa Workshop. Just wake up before the bins are emptied.'

The dark image of him curled up on a cardboard raft, sinking next to a glass room filled with sofas and beds, bites me quicker than the cold.

Our breath coils together a little longer. In a week, they will be thirty-six weeks' pregnant. Then they will be given a B&B room in a crack den. He was clean in prison and he can keep going. I ask him to wait. I turn to Annie who has been hovering back a little from us.

'Give me a sec?'

'Of course.' She knows what I am thinking before I do. She's thinking the same thing, just at what she considers a safe distance. 'Meet you back here.'

We part. She goes to the nearest coffee house and buys them a hot drink and a meal in a bag. I get some money from the cash machine flashing festive greetings. It's four days before Christmas.

He welcomes the hot drinks and Kay stirs. I crouch close to him and we clasp hands. Unseen, I pass him some money folded up. We know how to distribute secrets. I pull my hand away and wish him luck. I ask him if he is OK with me reporting his situation to those that can help. He gives me permission and looks a little prouder of being given a choice. Of being asked.

I walk away and try not to look back. But of course I do. They gather their holdall and sleeping bags. They head towards the night shelter. When he opens the folded notes, he will see that they have enough until they are housed. I worry all night that I shouldn't have given him so much. That he might do something else with it. But I trust my instinct and gradually the urge to go retching to the loo gives way to gulping sleep. In flicker dreams, I fight the other instinct to go back, scoop them up, and bring them home with me. A Christmas story with a warmer ending than his.

I looked for him every time I was in town. I reported him to StreetLink in the hope he would be sent a keyworker. I had a terse reply questioning if he really was homeless. The place they slept in was 'too public' to be genuine. He wasn't homeless until I saw him again two months later. On his own, his skeleton looked skin-stretched tired. This time I went straight over to him. He stood up slowly under the weight of his story. Crushed by the loss of their baby, they were further swept away by becoming homeless again. No longer deemed a family, they were put back on the streets. We both crouch down. Unable to hold up under the strain of pretending this was humanly possible. Two impossible inhumans ignored by walking shoes chattering past.

Even in Dickens's time, they would place a foundling with a homeless couple to allow them to live in parish poor houses. What have we become? I get them lunch, which he will take to Kay, who is buried behind the shops. She can't face the light anymore. I don't blame her. I reach for my phone and report his position to StreetLink again. This time I get a response from the local charity in the area. They know him. They tell me they will send out a key worker to collect them. It's all I can do. And I hate myself for walking away. Even though he has long gone back to wake Kay with news of a meal and a roof to sleep under. Sleeping at night is a rare treat. A chance to rest vigilant eyes and ears. We share that.

An email comes too late to mend my flashback dreams. It tells me they are OK and they are being supported. But my head and heart have already broken. Splinters cut through my chest wall. Razor wire dreams, if I'm lucky.

No sleep. Arrive early. Walk in with officers. Smiles fade. Breathe in. Get spat out of airlock. Collect keys. Pick up radio. Check battery. Low. Change battery. Halfway. Change battery. Full, third time lucky. Bang gate shut. Check gate. Unlock next gate. Check it. Check it again. Smirks – theirs not mine. Walk to unit. Drink coffee. Share jokes. Hopes. Fears. Hear the previous night terrors. Leave unit. Go to meeting. Hear more fears and hopes. Bang gate. Switch radio on. Earpiece bites. Check gate. Walk to the wing. Wait. Alarm. Stand back. Wait. Stand back. Stand down. Take a stand in the classroom.

Perhaps today will be different. Nothing is normal anymore. What will we add to the rotating mix of hilarity, routine, shouts, words, silences, nudges, side-eyes, joy. Oh joy. Another alarm. Next door. I wait inside the room. Arrange sticky sick tables. Find enough chairs with four legs. A legless zombie man is escorted off the wing. Search for hooch and Spice. National security has descended to delay unlock for another half an hour. They narrow-eyed stride in. They leave empty-handed, grumbling at time ill spent.

Wipe tables and slates clean. Bored of cleaning, board sits waiting. I walk out, down metal stairs, and into the office. Sign in and collect all the orange folders I recognise. There are other names in my head to watch over. Ridiculous. They watch over me. Keep me going. Stop me from getting lost under the overwhelm. Waves of papers, old TVs, radios, rocks, and fossils. Old books and silent stories untold. Here there is nothing. Nothing but people. None of the stuff and nonsense we hide behind. Nothing to prop up our sense of self. Equals in breathing, living stories. I can't think about the one who is only living in my head.

I welcome the smell of burnt toast and weak coffee coiling up the landing. No ghosts behind the yellow doors. I can see half-faces waiting behind them. The vertical glass panel is too narrow to see them all. Muffled words ask when we can meet face-to-face. Raised voice says soon. Unlock is delayed until all the counts are in. A series of numbers are relayed. They don't add up. Nothing does here. Always an odd number, unbalanced, and off-kilter. Try again. Roll check. Heads will roll. Eyes in the back of your head.

Release. Breathe out. Wait until all the men have gone to work or classes. Now the rest are put back in their place. Some float on the landings, fetching buckets and water for their cleaning jobs. An officer checks who has signed up for my workshop.

'Fourteen. Here's my list.'

'Really? With just you?'

'Yes. Just me. And them.'

'Even him?' He points to a name.

I know what his now tight lips are saying. A danger to women. Known staff assaulter and racist. He has already been flagged up as someone with complex needs. Someone whose record doesn't make it easy to empathise. He needs more than my words can give him. So we'll look at his. He's quite a writer, weaving stories around the realities of his childhood. All contained in metaphor, we know what they mean. This poem was born in a crack den, surrounded by sleeping sex workers who couldn't afford to attend parents' evenings. There are some subjects I have to avoid. Like why I can't let him sit near the others or near me. Why he needs to stay seated and not move between me and the doorway. The others know, too. They don't know I know, wishing I didn't. Working for the prison means knowing what glances mean. Glaring light of understanding. The weight of silence strung between sightlines.

'Yes. I have a radio. It's OK.'

'We can check in on you if you want.'

'Thanks. But I'd rather you didn't. Unless you come in and write. That's the rule. I'm on a radio. I can call if I need to.' Fully charged and ready to go. Familiar finger tingling, stomach swirling, burning rising.

'OK.'

He trails down the list. He has to unlock each of them, scattered around the spurs. Wild West scenes set up and gathered for a showdown of games and stories.

His eyes stop again.

'Him? As well as all the other one?'

'Yes. Simultaneously, together, and at the same time. If he wants to come along, that's fine. He needs to be engaged in something. He wrote a long chapter ahead of last week. Hopefully it kept him out of trouble.'

'Hmmm.' He was quieter. 'Have you got charge in that radio?'

'Yes. When can you let them out?'

'Now, I guess.'

He strides off, jingling his keys. The men hate that noise. It reminds them of where they are. Even though they have their own cell keys on this wing. It's enhanced. Toilet next to where they eat. No way to keep a lid on the germs. Wafer thin, blue, washable mattress. Pale blue cellular baby blanket unless they had a duvet sent in. Kettles on high shelves, which don't reach the plugs. Given shortened cables. This is a vulnerable prisoner wing. Other things are missing. Hot water wall unit. Pool cues. No balls. Spice smog. Yells and thundering upstairs. Whoops of laughter. Here it is calmer. More serene. Men gathered on seats outside cells. Drink coffee in dressing gowns before work. Notes on wing meetings circulated. A community feel creeps under doors and through cracked observation panels. Names are left by doors. Notices still hold their own on the boards. Very bored now. Nothing to do but wait. The weight of the world outside is beginning to sneak in. Bare walls remind me of the final rooms now the boxes sit next to my bed. A functional skills poster asks if I have a function. I can do nothing but function. One foot in front of the door. Skip lunch. Sleep in my soup. Always alert. Screaming ears at night that TV white noise covers in a veil of half-light. Keeping watch in a silent house until I leave and return. Holding secrets is easier than letting go.

The sights find their way into words. Disguised as stories and poems of wilderness cities. The weeds are taking over. Coiling up the concrete and splitting the bricks. Shitting bricks spitting dust.

'Morning, Kate. Good to see you, Miss.'

'Hello, Will. How are you doing?'

'You remembered my name. I'm OK.'

'And you remembered mine.'

'So what are we doing today? More stories? All we do is tell stories.'

'Well, there are options today. We'll wait for everyone else to crawl in and then vote on it.'

'Fair play. Shall I put out the pens 'n' that?'

'Thanks, yes. That would be a big help.'

One by one they come in. Laughing about the rough night.

'Yelling and singing like a drunken pirate, he was.'

'Glad I'm on B spur.'

'I could happily push him overboard.'

'OK. Settle down. You know how I feel about threats.'

'No need to go overboard, Kate. See what I did there? Only joshing.'

'I know. But in here, words mean something. They can get you on a charge. What I say to my kids when I try to get them to clean their rooms would get me extra days here.'

'They messy?'

'Practically a dirty protest.'

We vote between writing a group story or using objects to create a story. They like choosing between things. Asking for ideas causes chaos, anxiety even in the longer stayers.

After hearing Arthur's poem, we get to work. Arthur recites the same poem from his time on the building sites. Taught to recite it as a way of passing the time, he is propelled back there for a while. Every week it's a triumph to hear it complete. The others silently listen and smile as he finishes. Or silently exhale if he doesn't remember the end. Dementia is taking away his words and serving time is not helping. His decline is rapid. He speaks of other times. Of family that are no longer alive, shifting sands of time between before it happened and now. The event that I know. The one slipped through the cracks in time spent out of the light. We meet at the beginning of my day and the end of his. Nocturnal wanderers. I measure my weeks by the words he has lost. We're in week twelve. We've lost the whole of the last verse now.

We begin with a game that helps everyone, me included, to tap into that creative part of the grey matter. The one that hides within every grey tracksuit around me. Here, some are wearing their own clothes. Another marker of time spent, privileges earnt, systems known, and cycles repeated. One particular student has been known to wear very little. Strutting in just his shorts. And as he sits down, we can all see they are boxer shorts. Mouths are not the only thing gaping.

'Ashley.'

'What, Miss?'

'It's not Comic Relief today.'

'And?'

'You'd best put that away. You'll frighten the horses.'

'Eh?'

'Fine. I'm done being subtle and you know it. In your hurry to get dressed this morning, you didn't. Best get dressed, eh?'

Pause.

I've moved to the other side of the room. Face firmly fixed upwards. No wandering eyes here. The others side-eye the way out. Narrowed eyes all round. Normally I'd ask him quietly to leave but that's exactly what he wants. For me to lean over him and get a mole eye full. It's too early in the morning for this. He's known for flaunting his wares at female staff. And we all pretend to not know what he's in for.

He grins. His chair scrapes across the worn floor and it only takes a quick granny-ginnel narrow stare before he is gone.

Three rounds of Pictionary later, they have all used the board, shared triumphs and failures, and now have three random objects in a list. Even better, we are all dressed, hot drinks over without being over anyone else, and the newly-returned Ashley's only streak is a winning one. Of course, I have had to take out all the triggering words: ones with double meanings for prison speak and euphemisms. We're left with not many vegetables or low hanging fruit. Playing cards, money, luxuries are also gone. A rationed world of the hungry.

'So what do we all have?'

'Cake, saucepan, and bat.'

'Bed, pond, and tree.'

'Flower, TV, and pen.'

'Hat, brush, and dog.'

No penis-shaped pens, snakes, or aubergines.

'We are getting somewhere now. Making progress even.'

'What do we need next for a story?'

'Somewhere like a setting.'

'OK. Think of a place. Write it down on the Post-it note in front of you. Done? Now pass it to the person on the right.'

'Damn it, Kate.'

'The fucking moon!'

'Better than Brixton.'

'My yard.'

'So what else do we need?'

'Maybe a time?'

'OK. You know the drill. Write down a time on the next Post-it note. It could be next week, last year, 1857. Go for it. What have you put?'

'Yesterday.'

'Today.'

'Tomorrow.'

'Now give it to the person on your left.'

'For fuck's sake!'

'Ha! Nice one.'

'Now for your final element. What else do you need? To help with the plot?'

'We've lost that long time since.'

'Nah, she means that style thing . . . you know?'

'Oh, like porn?'

'Or western?'

'That's the one. Genre. We talked about it last week.'

'Like the lesbians on a train?'

'Bit niche. So write a genre on the last Post-it note clinging to the table. Be inventive. Push it.'

Mischievous smiles. The sound of scribbling sent down rivers.

'What have you got?'

'Vampire western.'

'Horror musical.'

'Space romance.'

'So you remembered the hybrid idea then. Cracking stuff. So which way do I choose for you to hand it to?'

Hands hover. Mischief smirks.

'Actually, you get to keep them.'

'Oh fuck.'

'A thriller comedy on the beach from last week. Including a basket, cup, and radio.'

'Challenge accepted.'

'What did you get, Kate?'

'I have a blanket, cake, and magnifying glass on Mars. Comedy western in Roman times. I mean, how difficult can that be?'

'Good luck with that one.'

Furious scribblings scuttle under the voices in my ear. *'Alarms on E wing. Code Blue.'* Blue, black, and white blur past. We've either got used to the rushing about or are so engrossed that we don't see the dangers on the side-lines, lurking in the wings ready to take flight. Time to take centre stage. Monologues of imagined worlds, held objects, and times gone by. No one chose the future. Do we not dare hope? Or is it giving away too much of ourselves? Setting up to fail. Stories of lords meeting spies on bridges, wanted men running from the law, innocence and guilt marked on paper. Plots with twisted endings, set on stony faces as they realise we are nearing the end of the session. I've already warned them I am taking a few days off.

'Might do that again. Amongst ourselves, like.'

'I've left some materials in the office for you. Ask Officer B.'

'The one that talks like you?'

'Aye. The fabulous Northerner.'

'By gum.'

'Something like that.'

'Are you off now?'

'Not quite. A few people to see before I leave.'

'Not quite escape time yet, Kate.'

After the room has become the moon, a lift, a hospital, and other worlds away, it takes me a few seconds to remember where I am. Walking out of the door to encounter a former student soon reminds me. He isn't happy to see me, either. Glowers. Heartbeat. And then walks away. I go in the opposite direction, onto a different landing spur. I need to find six particular men. My virtual reading group and a couple of self-isolators. I know exactly where they all are. Each cell is marked with a card bearing their name. Cards marked already. Doors shut and locked from the inside. Hiding from eager debt collectors. Prices on their heads or double deals for canteen treats. Or worse.

I knock on each door. Then look through the panel. Some are illegally blocked off. Most come to the door and peer around the gap. A slice of human contact. I shake hands or fist bump. Their choice. Hand them some words to block out their sentences. Ask if they are OK. Do they need anything? Check in. It took me six weeks to get Alex to talk to me. Three just to speak. Two to make eye contact. Eyes lowered, he took the papers. Then, gradually, the words began. One at a time. I found out he was writing a song. We passed verses under the door between meetings. Early bang-up never helped. But seeing his face is a step forward. He is keeping his head down, literally, before release. Clammy hands post books back through the door gap. Gate anxiety and more. Moving from one place to another. Mustard door to white fire doors. Approved premises. Pending further investigation.

Looking into the next cell, I am greeted by Dave, my wing husband. Throwing down his Xbox controller, he welcomes me with a grin. Eyes lower than usual. Clouds on the horizon.

'You OK?'

'I'm OK. Want a coffee?'

'No thanks. Do I need to ask you again? Not prying, but you know I am. I know that look. Anything I can help with?'

'Review coming up. Need to take my mind off it.'

I've seen this haunted face before. The ghost hope of release held back by the fear of cycling back into old haunts and habits. The privilege of an impending visit weighed with pressure to bring drugs in. Sometimes it is better to stay still. Moving forward can mean going round in circles. Self-sabotage or contraband coercion. I'm not sure. Again, I feel that conflicting wish to both hear his voice talk with pride about his family and to never see him again. Not in here. For him to be with them. Transport them all somewhere outside the whirlpool of connections and contacts which pulled them under.

'You steering clear of the Spice still?'

'None come in anyway. Not that I've seen.'

'Are you still wing cleaning?'

'Not as much shit as usual. The one last week was the worst.'

'Worse than the education bogs?'

'Not that bad, mind. At least they'd spell the words right.'

'I'm not sure I want to know, but what words?'

'He'd written stuff on the walls.'

'More shit poetry?'

'No, not your man in the seg.'

'Ah, you knew him?'

'Yeah. One of your men. This wasn't him. This one was some fucked-up shit.'

'Want to share it and lessen the load?'

'Could do.'

Pause. We wait.

'You'd best tell me, then. Let me carry it for a while. But you also know the drill. If it's bad, I'll be reporting it.'

'I know.'

We perch on the edge of his bed like teenagers sharing after school secrets. Sitting next to him means he doesn't have to make eye contact. It makes it easier to talk and listen.

'So. How bad was it? Worse than last week's protest? Is it a double-bagger?'

'And some. He'd smeared blood on the walls.'

'Bloody hell.'

'Hell and a lot more besides. N words. Terrorist stuff.'

'Did you get support after seeing it all?'

'I got more bicarb and double bubble. Can't say fairer than that.'

'I could say a lot, but I won't.'

'That makes a change.'

'So now what? What do you need?'

'Could do with something to fill the evenings. Take my mind off. Fill in the gaps.'

'I can give you some writing, games, engagement stuff. Actually, I found a great tattoo book the other day. Just don't go getting a prison tattoo.'

'Much appreciated. You doing OK?'

'Am OK. Will be off for a few days, but I know Anna will check in, too. I will drop those extra things off later.'

'Cheers, Kate. Safe.'

Fist bumps. Smiles. Then he follows me out and sits down on the frayed blue chair on the landing. Being brought outside his cell, he is met by his friends. The other gentler faces from my sessions. Tough enough to survive, still furrowed enough to look out for others. I leave him there, chatting, the pack of papers still in his hand. At last count, he was released to DCat and hasn't come back into the system. Perhaps I will see him again on the outside. If we can both stay away from the prison luring us back with its promises of safety and familiarity. We know where we are there. Someone and nowhere. Lost and found in the in-between.

I'm clumping down the stairs of C spur and trying to not to slip on the ketchup-bean-slime trails signalling lunch. Mitch stops dead in front of me. Serious eyes. You probably wouldn't like to meet him on a dark night. I wouldn't. That would mean he had slipped through the chinks of light to become homeless again.

'Miss.'

'Yes?'

'You need to put your cardigan on.'

'Ah, fashion tips from the wing catwalk! I thought you didn't like my grannywear.'

'I don't.' He nods downwards. Trying not to look directly at the bloodstain. 'You might want to cover that up, Kate.'

I look down. Crapola. There's blood on my top. And it's from the inside out rather than the normal splatter accident. A small splotch of dark red claret sits on my chest. I'm actually bleeding. A broken heart blood pool hovers over my chest. I hastily cover it up. Pretend it was a nosebleed. We both know it wasn't. But neither of us knows what it is. Not yet.

I murmur a thank you and fold my arm over. Clutching a buttonhole and the bannisters, I try to style out my exit off the wing. I'm handed a roll of paper containing stories to look at. I move between the grey sea of men loitering at the office doorway asking for loo roll, phone credits, and plastic cutlery. Here they have to ask. There aren't any dignity bins.

I leave the unit. I graduated from the university of crime. No cap or gown. No fanfare. No speech. No cheers. A lone tin thrown in the air as I pass the last wing before the gates. The rooks are hovering. Vultures hoping for scraps. They scuttle towards the tin, flapping at my heels. I don't heal quickly. The blood crust has spread onto the paper stories I hold close. A sticky seal on a leaving message of returning hope.

13.

'Please take a seat. There's an order of service on the chair. We'll begin shortly.'

Dean's picture looks back at me. Slightly furrowed, squinting in the sun. I clutch the edges of the paper, gripping the words celebration, growth, memorial. The chair is prickling rough through my skirt. I push back into it. A hundred raw threads stab back. I'm hemmed in now. Anna is on my right, Liz to my left. Paper planes float to the ground under the seat in front.

'Here you are. These yours?'

His eyes look back at me, smiling.

'Thank you. Sorry.'

'It's alright, love. You're welcome.'

I choke silent coughs. The waves are washing over my feet. Washing away the mud from my boots. Seep sliding through the lace holes. I'm slowly drowning in salt water.

Mitch reads a Taoist poem. The words swirl around the prayer flag and coil up through the skylight.

Then one by one we speak. I don't notice until I stand up

that the room is monochrome full. Few grey tracksuits and only five of his peers. Either quickly forgotten or never held close. The glimpses of darkness are coming closer, pushed by jealousies trying to lure him back to them.

Susan speaks of his spark. His contribution to hope and growth, her project, which has held men between the two worlds and continues to nourish. What I failed to do. It jars my spine straight and I'm up on my feet. Lurching to the front. I see Mitch at my shoulder and he straightens up, smiling the words 'I'm here in case you fuck it up'.

'It's hard to know where to start – how do you sum up a character as large as Dean? Do I start with my first memory of his loud laugh – one that signalled his presence in the building long before he appeared in the room? Or do I end with the image of someone full of hope at the prospect of being an artist on the out?

'He was certainly larger than life, and a complex character. Fiercely loyal. Often with glitter under his fingernails. Passionate about people, yet the quiet soul of an artist. Positive about the angels who showed him a life without drugs, but who still spoke of glimpses of darkness. A wide smile and a wanderlust around the estate. The first to arrive and the last to leave. The generous nature that created art pieces, yellow stars, and wise words. I have so many of these stories of angels, demons, and light. So it seems fitting that last night I found one of his offerings. Not a large canvas of colour and light in his developing, deepening style. But a small, copied out poem by Khalil Gibran, which he wrote out in different coloured pens, with some added glitter stars, which he said would make me smile. So, from him to us:

"And in the sweetness of friendship

Let there be laughter

And sharing of pleasures

For in the dew of the little things

The heart finds its morning

And is refreshed.'"

I'm not sure how I got back to my frayed chair. It connects me to the ground. A head in front of me turns and his eyes meet mine again.

'Thanks, love.'

I can only smile back at his mother. A petite, wiry lady who had given him her heart, soul, and green eyes. I can't swim in them for long as the governor is speaking now. Words of sorrow and respect. That Dean had made a choice that we wish he hadn't. That we had to respect that choice and remember how we shared the journey. Saltwater waves are washing over me again. Arthur is pinching his nose and staring at a spot on the floor.

The dust catches the light, spiralling upwards towards the skylight. We're all just flickering dust.

Helen, one of the chapel assistants reads out the poem 'Invictus'. I have a copy, decorated in Dean's rainbows, on my classroom wall. The final verse hits heart home, eased by Helen's soft M&S drawl. This isn't just poetry; this is luxury William Ernest Henley poetry.

'It matters not how straight the gate

How charged with punishments the scroll

I am the master of my fate

I am the captain of my soul.'

Next, an uplifting show tune. Hopping from glum to glee. Dean flickers into view. Without his body overcoat to frame the scene, he is able to flit between words and hover in the ache spaces between.

Ahmed and Miss P – strangers now friends in loss – read out some of his scrawled stories. They stand together and share the load, the push and pull of Dean's angels and demons.

Liz strides up in her Smarties Vans. Sighs out the struggle and begins.

'A green-eyed man, a curly hair'd boy . . .'

We're all falling. Puckered and leaking.

Anna scoops us up with a traditional blessing for a journey and we're left with the chaplain's final farewell.

'Dean, we are glad that you lived, that we saw your face, knew your friendship, and walked the way of life with you. We deeply cherish the memory of your words, deeds, and character. We leave you in peace. With respect we bid you farewell.'

Between clenched teeth I mouth the final Irish blessing. It shouldn't end with the standard plug-and-play words I've heard four times already this year. Dean didn't fit into a template. None of them did. That was part of the problem. Platitudes in place of a funeral. Fit for nobody. I know rituals are meant to be comforting. But here they lose their purpose. No body to witness leaving. Here there is no leaving. No curtain to draw. We're left haunted.

I don't want to go to the tea and biscuits after. We're surrounded by Dean's silent art works. I want to rage and cry but that won't come until much later. We're caught between knowing and not seeing. It's not real if I can't see it. He still hovers in my phone, held outside in the other place. Where his son is. Where the what-might-have-been floats in the prickled dawn light.

Time to straighten up. Find some strength from cold bones. To stop gazing at one of his last paintings. A life-size image of a couple in a close embrace. Only his figure is faded, a ghostly soldier. Her lost love. She is caught in time. Freezeframe. Time to refocus. Because there's someone I need to speak to. The face with his eyes. His mum.

'I don't know what to say. I'm sorry. I miss him.'

'You knew him. Saw him. That's enough.'

'How are you holding up?'

'We can't have a funeral yet. There'll be an inquest, too.'

'I can't imagine.'

'He left a note.'

'I can imagine that, though. He was always covered in words or paint.'

'I'm keeping them all. His stories.'

'I've brought you some more. For later.'

'I've got a box. For Sam. For when he is older. He doesn't want it yet.'

'If there's anything I can do, will you let me know via Susan?'

'Of course, love.'

'May I . . . ?'

And before I finish, she is hugging me. Fiercely close. Until she becomes aware that the governor is waiting to escort her out. Visiting time is over. Memory box shut. Closed off.

'Kate. We're going to get a coffee. Coming?'

'Yes, thanks.'

Stirred up dark waters. No amount of sugar can lift this bitter bite.

'You OK?'

'Nope. Not yet. Not for a long while. Your words, Liz. Left me broken.'

'We'll carry it better in time.'

'Another lump of kit for the belt.'

'We might have to wear the cameras soon.'

'No chance. I'm out of here before that happens.'

Balanced tilted hips, walking between loss and life, we walk out together. Pretending it won't still ache as much on the other side of the gate.

14.

'How was the funeral? I can't see why you wanted to go in for that. You're supposed to be on leave. You wouldn't get me in there for love nor money.'

'I know, Lynne. Crap money anyway. And it was a memorial.'

'Well, it's over now at least. Did the dress fit?'

'Yes thanks. You'd have been proud of the matching belt. Felt weird, though.'

'It would do. You didn't borrow the original one.'

'No. I meant the day.'

'It's bound to. Who heard of a memorial for a prisoner?'

'He wasn't a prisoner.'

'Sorry, ex-prisoner.'

'Why do you say that? It's like ex-wife, ex-husband. He isn't what he was before.'

'You say the funniest things. Of course we all are.'

'I bloody well hope not.'

'And we all know where hope got you: prison!'

'Could you say that any louder? I think the table over there didn't quite catch it.'

The waiter scurries up with the bill and holds the card reader at arm's length. Contactless. Apt. Distance maintained. Just how I like it. How I need it.

'Oh stop fussing. Got us the bill quicker, didn't I?'

'At my expense again. Well played.'

'Oh I think you'll find you've been played, my dear.'

All that manipulation training for nothing. Lynne's eyebrow raises. Lynne, I'm not giving you any more ideas. You're already platinum level. And I need to get back. I've got to buy more pens and Vanish on the way home.

Walking through crowded city streets, listening to inane chatter, pinging phones, murmuring traffic, the noise of Saturday leads to sounder sleep. The ringing in my left ear is a constant reminder of the radio waves beckoning me back. Shop alarms shudder me out of the quiet. I can hear the voices. Assistance required. The men talking over them, carrying on unknowing. But Saturday. That's the day after Friday comedown. A night of sleep with no work to wake to. A brief glimpse of what lies outside the gates. Until they cave in. Memorials for men months gone. Dead fathers. Carrying the corpses clinging to the edges. Blood-lined nostrils. Sweet-smelling Spice before the screams shudder to silence. Life drained before my eyes.

Standing in front of the mirror, I hold up the four dresses needed for the next onslaught. Must remember to ask my ghosted husband to drill another hole in my slipping belt. All present and correct. No splits or stains. Hanging right side out. Not falling for that again. Remove the belts. Hang up my belt. If I forget it, I have to grovel to security for another. And they do love giving me the one which could go twice around Santa. Four pairs of leggings alongside. Layers of safety and cold comfort. The same flowered boots will make their rat stomp each evening. No coat unless it's arctic. Too much to grab in the event of a hasty exit. Too many pockets to search. Less time for morning coffee. A line-up of blue dress, the unknown gap where a dress should be, red dress, blotchy dress, black dress.

Mediterranean blue dress wriggle washes over brittle morning bones. Time to put on my big girl pants and get on with it. My work husband is waiting patiently at the gate. He's offered to take this week's driving. He knows what's waiting tomorrow. He makes out it suits him to carry this lift share. We both pretend we haven't seen the bloodstains at the end of the day. By now, I'm bleeding through pads that are slip sliding down with the weight. Words like oncology and breast cancer haven't been spoken yet. All I will acknowledge is that three hours of lessons without a break are too long, so I've negotiated only going onto the wings. Like that's an easier option.

'Mornin.'

'That it is. Not necessarily a good one. But one all the same.'

'You good?'

'Always. Well, maybe not always. But today, yes.'

'You never can give a straight answer.'

'Have to keep up the word count, you know.'

'I think I prefer the silent type.'

'You love it really. Got much planned for today? Aside from the standard merry-go-round that is.'

'Looking forward to a lunch over at the kitchens. Brought in a pile of pizzas. Lee is making puddings.'

'Not just desserts, then.'

'The full shebang. What about you?'

'Back on the wings and then the seg, for my sins.'

'You still coming for lunch, though?'

'If I can get something to bring on the way?'

'We'll stop off at the shop.'

An hour later I'm clutching a pile of crisps, a block of cheese, and six different newspapers. The cashier greets my illicit stash with a wry eyebrow rip curl. She can see my work belt and knows where I'm headed.

'What kind of day are you expecting with all that lot?'

'Junk food lunch and teaching media. Standard heady mix. Have a good day.'

'And you. Take care.'

The kindness of strangers always puts me on edge. They can see it. The danger. The things we laugh off. The moments we have come to think of as normal. Without knowing, she sees what I'm walking into. The hurly burly of the wings. Rows of open doors. Hold my breath. Don't inhale the Spice smoke. Sharp breath sting of vape. Intake before holding together a wrist. Breathe relief at seeing Dave's smile. Breath knocked out as shields storm past. Breathe relief. Breathe. In and out of each cell on the upper landing. On my uppers.

'We good?'

'Let's do this. What can possibly go wrong?'

John puts the food haul into his bag. He carries it in as if it's as light as the change of clothes I'll need by breaktime. As light as the air we cannot breathe. Keys collected. Radios hooked in. He holds the gate open and we go through the grim portal. The air is heavier. Mist is clinging to the fences, wrapping its veil round the blocks. Nothing to see here.

One by one, we arrived. Sink into frayed chairs, wonky frames settling into the same morning.

'Coffee?'

'Yes please.'

'Someone's nicked my cup again.'

'We're running out of milk again.'

'Who've you got in today?'

'H Wing's library day. Prepare for a kick-off. Jones has been banned again but he'll be at the door. Too much of a pain in the arse to keep on the wing.'

'What was he banned for this time?'

'Writing.'

'Serious crime indeed. It's how I ended up in there, after all. But really, spill the beans.'

'We found his book on one of the computers.'

'He'd nearly finished at last count. I'd edited his pitch. So what was so bad?'

'Did you read all of it?'

'Yes. We took out a couple of references to keep him safe. We've talked about making it into a novel.'

'So he fooled you too, then.'

'Meaning?'

'Spot any gaps in his story?'

'Trick question that one. There are gaps in everyone's stories. Stop arsing about, Bill. Be a lady and spit it out.'

'Charming, Kate. The page gaps.'

'There were a couple near the beginning. He's only just learnt to use Word, so I figured he needed to reformat?'

'You could say that. His book starts as a porno.'

'What the fuck?'

'Exactly. Those gaps weren't spaces. He'd written it in white.'

'Holy crap.'

'Security went apeshit. The college are now looking into it.'

'I bet they are.' A couple of dirty grins.

'Actually, it's pretty serious.'

'How bad?'

'Depends. If they find who was on duty when he was typing it, they will get fired.'

'Seriously? Hardcore reaction for what?'

'Oh I particularly liked the description of multiple partners.'

'Is that all? I mean in some religions, that's expected.'

'Well you're a dark horse, Miss!'

'Nope. Just a one-track pit pony. Just seems like an over-reaction. Was there anything illegal in what he was describing?'

'No.'

'I'm not sure how I feel about this to be honest. I think I am more pissed off because he forgot all I taught him about metaphor. Walk into a cherry orchard and John Thomas is your uncle. Censorship avoided. But then here we are. No room for manoeuvre. Even a funny look can get you on a charge or fired.'

'So remember that with your one-to-ones. I wish you wouldn't go onto the wings.'

'You're not the only one, Bill. But it's not as bad as you think. Perhaps you could come along one day.'

'Jesus, I'd rather have six wives.'

'That relies entirely on you finding five more women foolish enough to marry you. How many trial runs have you had now?'

'Fuck off already, cheeky.'

'And fuck you too, my dear. Although I wouldn't touch you with John's.' I curtsey, smiling, and wash up all the cups ahead of the morning. I'm still thinking about Jones as I walk onto the wings.

Here are all the spaces, the washed-out words, and the missing. Some deliberately hidden from view, all kept away from you. Tucked up in bare rooms, walking grey areas of part truth, part lies, under thin blankets and over-anxious. They are milling around before bang-up. Trying to catch the light through the wider canteen windows before going behind their doors. The smell of toast caught in the grill filters through cracked observation panels as they are pushed back inside. Some crawl back into bed. Others get ready for work or classes. The wing cleaners, laughing, gather metal clanging buckets of empty nothings to pass the time.

I step over a pool of murky water swilling out of a cell. Seeping secrets of a bad night pull back from my toes as the heady combination of blood, sick, and weak cleaning fluid washes over my face.

'Sorry, Miss. I'd give this spur a miss for a while if I were you.'

'Thanks, Mitch. I know you'll have it ship-shape soon enough.' Pause. 'Is he OK?'

'Been moved to the VP wing. Proper mashed up.'

'Poor sod.'

'Did it to himself. Found him clinging to the wall. No idea where he was. Blood, puke, and piss everywhere. Had to explain he was inside doing bird all over again. Some folk never learn. Imagine starting all over again. First week's the worst.'

'More work for teachers, eh?'

'They don't stick around long. Why do you do it, Kate? We ain't worth it.'

'Because I happen to think you are. What's the L'Oréal tagline again?'

'Because you're worth it, Kate.' He grins. 'Do you ever let up?'

'I don't know how to.'

'I feel sorry for your husband.'

'Why's that?'

'He gets what's left. I ain't seen you take a proper holiday yet.

You'll be in weekends soon. Is it true you were in Christmas Eve?'

'Liz and I did a wing tour with some paper, envelopes, and the like. Oh, and her dog.'

'Aw man, I miss my dog. Proper corker, he is.'

'What breed?'

'You won't like it. He's a Staffy. Loyal to a fault.'

'Did you know they were originally bred as nanny dogs to watch over children? Soft as owt but proper fierce towards anyone who threatened their charges.'

'Bit like someone else we know then, eh Miss?'

'I don't know what you mean.' My turn to grin. 'What's his name?'

'Here, Miss. I got his picture with me. This is my Max. Don't tell no one.' He pulls a photo from his pocket. Dog-eared soulful eyes look at me.

'He is a keeper. A walking story. Bit like someone else we know, eh Mitch?'

'Maybe, Kate. Say nothing.'

'Speak soon.'

I turn back for a moment. Catch a smile and put it on my belt for later.

'You missed a bit.'

'Haven't we all, Miss.'

My feet dry by the time I reach Manuel's cell. Right at the end of the landing, I know he's waiting. Where else would he be? Now comes the tricky part. Where I get to practise my best Spanglish. Between my Spanish and his English, we can order a beer, buy a train ticket, and swap obscenities. Fucking brilliantly useless. This week I am armed with a phrase book and all the prison app forms I can lay my shaking hands on.

'Hello Manuel.'

'Ah, Miss! How doing?'

'I'm fine thanks. And you? ¿Que tal?'

'Muy bien.'

Same lies in different languages.

First things first. The medical app. How to get an appointment. This one usefully has pictures to tick:

'Nurse.'

'Doctor.'

'Dentist.'

'Optician.'

'Pants. I get new pants?'

'Not quite. This is tricky.'

'Is trick pants? Like magic?'

'Argh! No! Eeerm. It means if you have a problem with . . .'

'With pants? Like how you say "skid marks"?'

'Oh dear God no. OK, here goes . . . Your willie. Little man. John Thomas. Nob?'

'It goes?'

'Oh Jesus. As in what's *in* your pants.'

'Ah. You mean "cock". Why you not say?'

'I shouldn't talk to a man in here about his cock.'

'Why not? What of it?'

'Because your cock is very much your business.'

'It not business. It lifestyle.'

'You did say you have ten children and four ex-wives. Anyway. You tick this box here if you have a problem with your cock.'

'Very good, Miss Kate. What is it next?'

'The canteen sheet?'

'Sheet? Like crap?'

'A sheet like this paper. You need this to order things. Like a shop.'

'Ah. I need. Tell me.'

'Shampoo.' I mime washing my hair.

'Soap.' My best Lady Macbeth impression.

'Bodywash.' Pause. Pause some more.

'Ah, Miss. For wash cock!'

Sound of jangling running. Two officers burst round the door. Officer bemused and officer worried. They leave having reassured themselves and worried Manuel.

'Miss.'

'Are you OK?'

'You not allowed here?'

'I will be here every day I can. Remember the days?'

'Mornday. Toosday. Wednesday. Tursday. Fryday.'

'What is today?'

'It Mornday.'

'So I will be here again . . . on Wednesday.'

'Am glad. I . . .'

I look at his face. Words on the tip of our tongues. Lurching silences. Then I remember. A cheap phrase book in my pocket. Between the dating section that moves from 'would you like to sleep with me' to 'I am busy' in three phrases and the directions to places we've both forgotten exist is what we need.

'¿Que necesitas?'

He sigh smiles.

'This.' Points at the papers and books spread across the blankets. 'Or I . . .'

Manuel turns his arms outwards. Amidst the rose tattoos lie his shredded arms. He makes the action of cutting. Quickly. Slicing. Cutting out the pain. Self-editing. Blank lines between blood blooms.

I nod. No need for words here. His split stories speak for themselves. All I can do is acknowledge them. Go beyond the scanning for new cuts, checking the room for blades and blood. I see you.

'I see you. Not tomorrow. Next day.'

'Yes. Next lesson is Wednesday.'

'Is good. I learn much. I buy toothpaste now.'

'Yes.'

'And cock wash.'

'Yes, Manuel.'

'Yes, Miss.'

He clasps my arm as I get up to leave. No fist bumps. A meeting of hands and arms cut by inked stories. Flowers entwined for a brief human moment. We know the blank spaces in between that speak of the hidden forbidden. Ghost stories and cracks to fall through. And I'm falling further. I see Dean's wide eyes everywhere. They're walking right through me as I move to leave the wing.

Given the panic I've already caused, it's best to sign out. I leave a message for the staff to keep an eye on two men who are falling too. Outside the window, chequered pasts appear in the glass squares. Sally rushes in for assistance as someone begins a cell barricade. He's threatening to hang himself. Again. As they leave, Josh walks towards the office hatch. I am mid locking up as he stops in front of me. He looks dead ahead and raises his hand to scratch his neck. Only he's slipped a piece of glass between his fingers. And he's cutting ragged chunks out of his skin. He's trying to slit his throat. Sally's returning flush of relief at averting the last crisis bleeds out of her face. She is behind Josh, meets my face, then the blood, and pulls his hand away so I can go for the jugular. No time for gloves. Keep your head. Hold his on. Now the throng takes over. Hands all over. Red, white, and blue hands holding him downwards until the nurses arrive. Soothing words and bandages. Move back. Push the rest back to their cells. Push it back inside my head. Deep inside to fuel the darkness.

Josh becomes an incident report, words scored onto paper before I leave. Trying to get the pen to work scrape-tears it up, and I have to start again. Turn over a new leaf. Leave with his blood on my hands and boots. It's just a flesh wound. But try telling my broken head that. It will speak of silent awakenings, flashforwards, and freezeframe wonderings if it will stop. Pillow-punching dawn hours, turning to face the silent face of a husband who has no idea.

15.

It's Tuesday. The unknown day. Inhaled by hospital doors, I struggle to breathe. No weighted belt to anchor me to the ground. Watched by uniforms. I've tried everything in the bag of tricks. Found five things I can see, four I can touch, three I can hear, two I can smell, and one I can taste. Screen, door, poster, desk, light. Leaflet, plastic cup, chair, leaflet. Nurse, crying, phone. Handwash, fear. Blood-bitten lip.

And this poem is still sleepless, shitting herself.

Panini press and biopsy sting. I'm holding a few more leaflets and waiting for the verdict. I've been moved from the bustle of a waiting room to another level. This room is quieter. The air smells different. Spaces between people sat on plastic chairs. Wider eyes. Hope has sunk to the lower levels of the building. I can't find the words. I don't like theirs. Tumours. Excision. I'm not explaining myself very well. That's now their job. Detail the source of the problem. I am deeply aware that they can see inside me. I can't mask anything. There is nowhere to hide. All the things I've covered over with papered stories. The numb sheen veneer of resilience. None of that armour works here. I'm stuffed in a small room and I'm under surveillance. Bed watch.

It's their job to explain what is happening. Write words for why my insides are seeping out. Demanding to be noticed. They refuse to be contained anymore. I've been bleeding for a couple of weeks. It won't stop. We can't pretend it's ketchup or pen or paint or jam anymore. My body has been keeping score, and now purple pen has marked the problem. I have failed this exam. I am no longer functional.

I've been poked and prodded and the smiles have stung the most. They always send the nurses in first to stem the blood. First aid for the heart. Murmurs around screens. They've seen beneath my skin. Sliced into the sides and kept, clicked, a little sample for later. Thin Steri-Strip tapes tug me together as I shrug back my trusty cardigan. I'm skin on bone. Paper-thin skin wrapped over exposed flesh. Crumpled around what should be smooth curves, falling short at the edges like a child-wrapped Christmas present. Just without the eagerness to open. Rather cover, wait for the healed underlayer to push through. A sticky, ripped rebirth left for later.

My phone keeps ringing. I know who it is. I can feel our panic doubled. Lynne has got stuck in traffic. Not moving forward. Me neither. And she's missing the show. We've done the unwilling volunteer and swords through a box trick. Now we're waiting for the magician to saw the lady in half. Sparkle sequin sweat and plumes of inner rage.

Only now it's me in the blood-stained grey joggers. Words

fall onto paper, re-writing the body with new whirling thoughts. Feelings of not feeling. Numb, in between possibilities. Everything else has more defined edges. Colours more vivid to pierce the senses. So sharp I can feel colour. Painful textures of fallen leaves crunching underfoot. Leaf people scurry past. Wincing steps taken to the tall glass and metal building which casts no shadow. Rustling old parking tickets, coins crashing, whining to produce the unwanted permission to stay awhile.

A letter stuffed in the pocket in case I forget where to go. If found, please return to Ward 33. A different sliding door sighs behind me. No survival belt. No black and white smiles to reassure me. The amateur-hour security guard's straight-face welcome. Radios are on. Batteries are low. As one door closes, there aren't any others opening. I'm trapped. Held in limbo. Breathless. I walk with tilted hips into the atrium. The well-mopped corridors that normally greet the poverty tourists shine underfoot. No voices in my head. Just screaming constant high-pitch tin-can ears, a wireline slicing the silence.

'Assistance required.'

Soft steps echo in the atrium. They know you're here and they are waiting for you. Thin smiles and knowing looks.

'Try not to worry'.

Which is exactly what I will do now, thanks. What shouldn't I be worried about? What is hanging in the air, mixing with the taste of alcohol gel? Not enough alcohol, methinks. So scrambled I can't even bloody spell it. I can smell it though, days after. Focus. Come on. Look at the posters. Study the curves and colours: pink, blue, and Macmillan green. Stare at the walls and corners. Black and white marks on the floors like a poor-man's version of Pollock. Pollock. Now there's an unfortunate name. But who am I to talk of misfortune? In that department my cup runneth over. Spilling, gurgling onto the ground to form a sticky, marbled pool of blues and browns.

'Kate Dulson, Room 2. Dr Giddens.'

An electronic voice drones out a name which doesn't match the one on the screen. Mispronounced, stressing the end letters rather the middle. Let's not get to the end just yet. If it doesn't sound like me, then it can't be my turn, right? Turn right at the first off-white corridor. Fuck. Here we are. The door runs up too quickly. It's ajar, attempted invitation. Nice try but I'm not falling for that.

'Welcome, Mrs Dulson.'

What does that even mean? Did I come in well? With the correct flourish of anticipation to set you at ease? Or a suitably serious tone, a dour shuffle of resignation?

'Please take a seat.'

Really? Good idea. Let's pick it up and go outside where the air of potential still hangs. It's been a few hours since you scanned my broken heart and squashed my boobs in your big sterile panini press. More like weeks of sleepless nights, darting from one distraction to another. That last time was a dozen box sets ago. None of the nurses are here now. I know what this means. This is the clinical part. I've piqued your interest now. There's something there.

'How are you?'

Do you actually expect an answer? I suspect not, but anything other than 'fine' might speak to the curled-up ball of pure fear nesting in my back. Gone as deep as it can go, stretching as far as a tingling finger's twitch.

'So it's as we thought.'

We? I was thinking this was all a horrible prank. A way of making someone realise all the things they hadn't done, what's important, and then allowing them the time to adjust life accordingly. To stay up all night talking, entwined. To write the lost stories, to find the ways to say sorry and I love you without making the loss so much keener. To pull my fingernails from the speeding car's dashboard and allow myself to leave. To trust all will be well.

'If you look at the body map it shows where we need to make the incision.'

Do we have to look at the left side? To think about what will be left? My left, your right. It doesn't seem right. Can't we turn around where possible? Recalculate. Take a diversion. Look at the stars and the sky one more time. Return to the hotel in the sky. Find that crumbling stone circle from long ago and go back. To a time without needles or sickening drugs. A time of not knowing. What are your thoughts on reconstruction? You have options. Such as? Press 1 for acceptance. Press 2 for denial. Press 3 for talking to God. Press 4 for other enquiries. It's your choice to wait until a later date or complete the next stage whilst you're already under.

'If we need to remove more tissue, then you can have reconstructive surgery later.'

We should rebuild. Once you've broken ground it seems uneconomical not to go ahead. How do you fill the grooves you've hacked away? Stretch tired, fraught skin over new flesh. Mounds that speak of what's buried beneath. A barrow to house the soul. One of silicone and plastic to far outlast the dead.

'Is there someone who can be with you? To help you decide?'

Are you kidding? I'm never alone. My ear is always burning. There's a heaving multitude inside me, turmoil voices of best intentions, quiet fearful pauses, held hopes, and enveloping love for what may come, to tackle together. And it's them who will look on what I have become. Of what remains after I have gone. So let them have their say. Perhaps we can take a vote. A democratic process of working through what they can bear to look at. Of what will allow them to look without pity or averted eyes. To stare back and re-member my body. A manifesto of what can survive and what cannot be spoken of again. A declaration of independence and a closing of the history book.

'You should be aware that you will most likely lose all sensation on the left side.'

I lost the ability to feel anything a long time ago. The moment that call came in. When I knew bone-deep he was gone. Of not being able to make up for lost time. Of losing the habit of getting up and going in without thinking. An autopilot response to cope with what lies within.

The next three dresses still hang on the door. I'm frozen-fall pitched into the next moment, clutching anger in an overnight bag. The quicker we get this edit done, the better. I've got a place to be. One where I float unfeeling between pinched sights. Back into numbness. Now my insides are clambering to spill out and I need to push it all back in before I go back. My skin is how I meet the world. It needs to hold me next to the rest. Be a boundary. I can't go back inside until I am whole outside. So they book the operation. Scribble marks on my body and paint it red with antiseptic wash.

'Sharp scratch. There we go.'

Blood pulses back.

'So what do you do?'

'I teach in a prison.'

'Wow. That must be a challenge.'

'No more than your job, I'd guess. Pale frightened people in pain. Occasionally violent. All needing help.'

'I hadn't thought of it that way. I mean I loved *Prison Break*. What's it really like, though?'

'There are plenty of tattooed men. And that's just the staff.'

My spreadeagled arm offers her flowers, a dragonfly, and a Manchester worker bee as evidence.

'Is it as horrible as they make out?'

'Depends who's filming. As soon as a camera goes in, everyone acts differently.'

'Aren't you used to them, though?'

'We don't have them in classrooms. I may have to wear one for going in the seg, but I'd rather not.'

'Really? I thought you'd have a guard.'

'Nope. The day I feel I need one is the day I leave.'

'Wow. So exciting though.'

'Sometimes. When a man passes an exam or leaves and doesn't come back. But I'm guessing that's not what you mean.'

'I meant the fights. We get a few in here. I used to work in A&E. Ugh! Friday nights were the worst.'

'Most days. Seen too many. Split up a few. Caused a couple. I'm used to it. Part of the game.'

'Our security guys are fab. Darren is my fave. He asked me out last week. Am playing hard to get for now.'

'Helps the response times, then?'

'Maybe.' Knowing smile. 'I'll be back in a few minutes to take you up to theatre.'

'Thank you. For taking my mind off it.'

Creeping cold seeps through the needle, pushing hard past thick skin into closed-down veins.

'There we go. Count down from ten.'

Ten . . . nine . . . eight . . . seven . . . still here . . . six . . . five. . . Years falling into numbness.

Stuttering images buffer between sinking. Stop-start spinning. Clinging to the walls as the bright light blur fades. Holding the edge of the trolley as I'm served up for the feast. A mangled meal of snakes and stories. I'm keeping all of them safe inside to protect the ones left behind. I'm trying to keep the box of all ills closed. Pull apart Pandora and hope escapes. It pulls others up through the cut. You aren't allowed tape in prison. So it all comes tumbling. Vinegar and brown paper tales of childhood traumas still falling.

The stomach-rising bile that stops me eating. Burning uprisings. Men yelling. Smoke smells and fire alarms blazing. I can hear the walls bleeping. Rushing out for the count. Dave's missing. Man down. Wing husband dashes out in a flurry of words and apologies. Mop still in hand. Jones scooped out of the library corners. This is not a drill. C Wing is alight. Alive with bodies. Skin seared faces, faeces smeared walls. I feel sick to my exploding stomach stench. Gloved hands hold me down. Pull me apart. Tear out the glimpses of dark matter. The black hole I call a heart bleeding out. I can't feel them tugging out what remains of the milk of human kindness. We're being turned inside out all over again. Adam's lines. Arthur's ether poem. Spinning stories. Flapping chickens being fed strawberries. Grey crowds clouding my judgement. Stone cold rubber pizza served on a boiling stew sticky day. Bile stung nostrils inhale oxygen tubes. Artificial air locked between keys there and here.

Breath stuck in my throat. Tears dry tucked in my eyes. Layer cake of memories piled in boxes and yellow bags. Catching breath on dragon days. Slipping through their fingers. Snowflakes on their tongues. You can taste the air. Crunch it between curled toes. Thorns inside flower boots. Grinding mud and plastic spoons into the tiles washed with bleach. They pretend to rise above the puddles of disinfectant seeping under doors. They cling, straightlaced, to feet ready to run. Built for getting out of the way. Not for comfort and support.

Soulless after a year, they were glued together by a man who knew where they'd been. He'd recognised both me and the pattern-laden boots as he looked over the counter. I was glad the counter forced us apart. He was back in the world, outside and moving forward. I might have hugged him otherwise. He had moved and I was stuck mid-performance. Pulling down hems laid bare.

Squeezing and pushing what remains back. Scarecrow limbs. Straw-stuffed entrails. Spineless. Squeezing him so tight the dust flies into the sunlit air. Catching fire and life leaves an ashen phoenix. Flap flying from the railings on the landings as the rooks fly. The ravens are leaving the tower. It's crumbling. Castle failing. The wall has been breached. Shore it up with the certainty of hope and resurrection. Paper plane unsent letters soar. Glitter contrails. Dean is flying alongside me. Ether words pulled from anaesthetic smoke and mirrors.

'I'm sorry. I want to stay and keep breathing, find the break I have been looking for for so long. I have stayed silent, let others be who they are whilst I stay true to myself. My new self is better and stronger than the old one. I have come from nothing and learnt that I own nothing and no one owns me. I know myself, who I am, the one who can see the darkness come and go. I have come through the fire, been thrown to the toothless wolves, come out the other side. All of these paths lead me to the same place. Where I am now. I need to find a place away from the noise, the people making demands, the expectations to be bad again, the expectations to be an artist. There is too much noise, shouting,

yelling. Too many questions. There is too much quiet, silence, not speaking, ignoring, ignorance. This place is full of opposites. I am this place. I am undefinable. They cannot know me as I am. I accept my chaos and broken pieces from the past. They are me; I am them. It makes me who I am. I understand that now. I have stopped seeing the glimpses of darkness; they are all around me, staying close to me now. I am ready to leave now. I want to let go. To become immortal and be everywhere, in all the places I haven't been yet. I will watch over all of the people who have understood me and leave the rest behind. It's time to go. I know that it will be hard for the ones I am leaving, I am not really going far. I am found, not lost. I begin again. I will be at one with the elements. I am the fire, the air full of ashes. Look for me in the stars. It's my time to shine now. See you in the sky. Bright halo lights to guide you.'

Fuzzy felt light begins to crispen.

'You gave us a scare there. Good to have you back.' She hovers under the halo. A tattooed midwife bringing me round. 'Has that ever happened before?'

Flicker of notes. Words of a first edition dance past. Folded under the clipboard. She sits back on the stool. Checks the lifelines.

Blinking out the darkness.

'Has what?'

'You have very irritable airways.'

'What?'

'If you have another op you need to remind them.'

'What?'

'Extra magnesium helped.'

'Sorry. What?'

'You stopped breathing.'

'For how long?'

'Oh, not too long.'

Groggy and red-blurred.

'Thank you. For bringing me back.'

'You're welcome. I'll stay for a while, though. In case.'

Mumbling murmurings of shocked starlings.

'You're ready to go back to the ward.'

Assistance required. Code Blue to Code Red. There's a dressing, standing out against the stained red skin. The antiseptic wash is more alarming than the blood. I'm wheeled back to the ward to stare at more painted brick walls. My every move is monitored until they tell me I can leave once I have peed. Getting up isn't easy. Waddling down the corridor is worse. Nothing. This isn't a piss take. Deadly serious, like an MDT. Waddle back to bed and wait. A pale blue cellular blanket and metal bed is more familiar than they know. Only this time, I am on the inside. Watched by uniforms. On the promise of an early release for good behaviour.

One golden ticket stream later and I am on my way down the corridor. Lurching to bile-borne sickness when a ward phone rings. Wince jump at the sound of closing fire doors behind me. I can't turn to check if I am being followed. The comforting hum of white noise in my ear masks the oncoming footsteps.

We leave another public building with me having left a part of me behind. Three tumours and a life sentence "you're all clear" later, I am back inside.

Being left in my own head for too long isn't easy. Dean's glimpses of darkness are still there, rising and falling like waves. They bleed through the dressings. Scalpel clean cracks in my armour. New-reminded empathy packed into a laundry bag. Is it easier to see those sights and be left to watch them climb the walls at night? Or to feel them and wrap them in a baby blanket? A present for later, unfurling in class when least expected. No gift bows included. A surprise in each layer. Pass the parcel from man to man until I catch it. Then pass it to the staff, the nurses, the night team, the incoming shift, and back to me in the morning. A few more layers peeled away. Each time the music stops, my face falls away. Will this be the last layer? The one where we find the truth. Whichever version is being told in spiral stories spun. It's easier to go back. To pretend it's normal to hold a man together as I fall apart. Bloody floors. Riots of laughter. Nothing in between. That's where the madness lies.

I've been exposed to what lies beneath my stitched skin. I've been where all the human beings are. I've held bloody wrists and bled through my clothes. I've lost sight of what felt real. Been pulled from the place which keeps fears from kicking down your door. Pulling men from railings and pushing back. Standing between passion and rage. A place of monsters man-made from boys. No chance of expulsion. There's nowhere left to go. Wide-eyed fear, fight, flight, freeze, or faint. Lizard brains slither through piss trails and kettle trials. Skin peeling, shed to show the same blood-burnt despair.

My ears are still radio scream ringing. My feet and head are still heavy, trying to keep away the rat gnawing thoughts. Flashbacks flicker on outer walls and ceilings, screens, and the pages of a waiting room magazine. At the beginning, I thought I would be able to tell the truth, the whole truth, and nothing but the truth. So help me, I lied. I haven't even given us all our real names. A final betrayal under the guise of safety. I want to speak his name. To let it roll out of my head and onto my tongue. I can't yet. It sits on the back of his paintings. Hiding from prying eyes behind water-washed-out colours clinging to the paper. But the rest is all true. To the best of my jigsaw knowledge. Putting it back together slowly here, through words, lines, and silences. Flashes, moments, too immediate to be memories. Too buried to be processed. Seen in pieces, seen from the side-lines, or right at the core. Burning lava, eyes leaking water to vainly put out the fires.

As I leave the hospital, I have the all-clear from Gold Command. I can stand down the worried friends, the strong, silent husband, and the anxious men inside. No further treatment needed. It's not aggressive and was well contained. Held in a duct, my milk of human kindness now removed. I have been invaded, poked, prodded, and cut apart with all the necessary pleasantries. A bit less of me is to return, recovered, and more aware of how precarious life is. A smiling scar to remind me of what the outside now knows. Now surfaced, my tangled fears and childhood memories need to be challenged. Put on a warning. To behave better or their privileges will be removed. Back on basic. Blank walls and behind doors again.

I approach along the lime walk towards the razor wire ringlets. I know it's different. The same routines make for a thin veneer. I'm seeing Lynne later. To talk of outer battle scars. My final warning written in black and blue ink has left me aware. Being drawn on, inscribed in ink, has put me back together. A treasure map of surgical marker. Insides folded within. Heart under layers of dressings, hidden from view. Not on the sleeve of my new dress layered on leggings and tights. Just under the surface, to be scratched by a rattle of tablets clattering down my throat to sit in an empty stomach. Weekly counselling visits sitting opposite another kind, strong, gentle man, who I'm afraid to spill stories to. Picking at the scab skin of moments past and present. Connecting stitches between inner and outer worlds. Putting the insides back. Blood-and-guts feelings from dangling men, scored arms and blue pale streets skin. Boundaries put back as the airlock slides shut behind healed skin.

It's all behind me now. In front, the door slides back. Slipping slowly into old habits. It's as easy as breathing. Radio. Keys. Gate. Coffee. Family.

'Release for Labour and Education.'

ACKNOWLEDGEMENTS:

I owe everything to the people who have to remain nameless – my prison family of teachers, officers, governors and men who taught me so much. The family and friends who found the patterns of light, the therapist who found the pieces and my husband who silently held it all.

My huge thanks to the people who in different ways encouraged this straggly bag of words to form into a story – M. J. Maloney, Rebecca D'Monte, Wyl Menmuir, Mim Skinner, Cathy Reizenbrink, Lucy English, Neil Samworth, Helen Woodhouse, Jonny Bainbridge*, Cassandra Rigg, Mark Thomas, Graham Hartill and most of all Darren Lee Floyd. The credit is yours, the mistakes are all mine.

* Follow Jonny Bainbridge on Instagram:
instagram.com/jonnybainbridge.art

ABOUT THE AUTHOR

Born in the North, Kate Dulson has clay and coal dust in her veins. Unremarkable, asthmatic and proudly owned by a dog named Casserole, Kate now lives somewhat mardily in the South with an ever-patient family.

After fifty foster dogs, five house moves, and twenty-five years of teaching and writing about other people's books, Kate Dulson left academia for what looked like nice regular college work. Arriving to see barbed wire fences, the job turned out to be in a Category C prison for men. That's when the writing started. Three years later, the living stories had spilled out onto pages of journals as therapeutic writing and some, quite frankly, terrible poems. Rather than inflict them on an unsuspecting public, Kate decided to rework the interwoven stories into a novel. After all who would read a memoir about a claggy working-class prison teacher with early onset bingo-wings?

Part autobiography, part silence, *Ghosted* follows Kate's prison education journey from her first lesson to the harshest lessons of all. It is haunted by the mercurial Dean, who also sees the glimpses of darkness. His imagined voice and very real glitter fingernails remain long after he has left. He shows how chance meetings can shape futures in strange ways. Just like the moment Kate met her future publisher up a mountain half-way around this world ago.

To discover more about Kate and her writing, please visit:

katedulson.com

To learn more about Stratosphere Books and join our newsletter, please visit:

stratospherebooks.com

Printed in Great Britain
by Amazon